The doorbell rang. Jeremy sighed. He was on the point of solving the final clue of that Wednesday's cryptic crossword in the Daily Mail. His target was to leave no more than three clues unsolved. On the occasions he succeeded in completing the entire puzzle he would use his iPhone messaging app to submit an entry. There was a £250 prize for one correct entry drawn at random. Over the past three years he had not been successful but he possessed an upbeat nature and today ... who knows? The doorbell interrupted his thoughts.

At first, he thought he had imagined the sound.

He lived beside a busy road and it was easy to occasionally misinterpret the source of outdoor sounds. Set inside its wooden frame, his front door contained a large sheet of dimpled glass. He expected to glimpse a blurred shape through the glass panel. He was disappointed. As he turned the key to unlock the door the bell sounded a second time.

"Okay, okay," he muttered and then, more loudly, "Give us a second!"

He turned the key and began to open the door. A shaft of the morning's sunlight caught him unawares and he raised a hand to shield his eyes. But he didn't close his eyes which was just as well or he wouldn't have seen the steel blade glinting in the hand of his visitor. He allowed his unwelcome guest to take a half-step into the hallway and then slammed the door in the man's face. It was a face with features he half-recognised, but on a far older man. The face he recalled did not have a broken nose. Blood dripped from the nose and onto the thin knife that his visitor had let drop to the floor. A small pool of blood stained his hallway.

"Who the hell are you?" Jeremy demanded.

"Who am I? I'll tell you who I am. I am Jacques Degarmo! My father would still be alive were it not for you and your daughter."

Jeremy stared at the young Degarmo in disbelief.

"Well, I never. How delightful and you've travelled all the way to England to meet me? Have you and idea what your father did in Paris last year?"

TWO

Six months ago, in the early days of spring, I had been sent to Paris on an assignment. I had met my contact at an unassuming structure on Avenue Marceau.

The building stood five storeys tall. Its corridors led to many other offices and one had a choice between winding staircases or a lift to navigate the floors.

The name of the man I had been sent to meet was

Emmanuel Degarmo and his office was on the third floor. I chose to use the stairs which allowed me the opportunity to gain an impression of the premises and its layout. I would have felt claustrophobic in the lift but then I've long harboured a fear of confined spaces Why? I'll tell you ... maybe later. Perhaps.

I was looking for a room without a number. I was told the door would simply bear a small tab with the initials' ED' in black against a white background. I didn't have any difficulty finding it although I had to walk the length of the corridor before reaching the door to his office.

I was about to knock but the door swept open whilst my fist was still mid-air.

"Monsieur Richards? Delighted to meet you. Did you have a good trip? Please come in and take a seat. I can't offer you any refreshments. There is no catering facility in this building, unfortunately."

"Monsieur Degarmo, I presume? Thank you for agreeing to meet me."

"It's always a pleasure to help my British friends … even when I have such a busy schedule," he added pointedly. "So, tell me ... why have you gone to the trouble of crossing the Channel to see me? Would a telephone call not have served your purpose?"

"I like to see the face of those I'm speaking to," I

replied. "A face can often tell me more than well-prepared words, Monsieur Degarmo."

"*Oui*. That is certainly true. So, what is my face telling you?"

"That you're impatient for me to explain the purpose of my visit."

"It's that obvious?"

Degarmo laughed and his features softened. "I'm all ears, as the English say,"

"I want you to find my daughter."

Emmanuel tilted his chin and looked steadily into my eyes for several long seconds before speaking.

"You think I run a lost and found department,

perhaps?"

"I think you have proved yourself good at hiding people. Are you as good at finding them, though?"

Emmanuel pursed his lips as he considered what I had asked.

"Possibly ... but then again ... maybe not. For one thing, it has to be possible to find them. I cannot find somebody who is slumbering on the bed of the Seine. Neither can I piece together a jigsaw of dismembered body parts. You understand?" I shuddered at the thought. It might have been kindlier of him to consider alternative possibilities. He must have read my mind, either that or he felt a glimmer of remorse.

"But, of course, that is most unlikely. Come, take a seat. Tell me about your daughter ... why you think she is in France, the reason for her being here and what it is that makes you fearful for her safety. Many young people visit Paris. It is a beautiful city, a city of romance, is it not?"

"It wasn't romance that brought her here. She is a keen historian and photographer. She has her own flat in Bristol and is a capable and self-sufficient young woman."

"Her age, monsieur?"

"She is twenty-two. I've brought along several recent photos of her."

"Oui, oui, in due course. Tell me more about her. Has she been to Paris before? Does she have acquaintances in France? Why do you consider her to be missing?"

"Sarah is twenty-two but already a seasoned traveller. She texted me eight days ago to say that her boat had docked at Calais and that she had collected a hire car from the port."

"Has she driven a car in France before?"

"Is that important?"

Emmanuel shrugged his shoulders. "I cannot know what is important until it becomes so. In England, you drive on the left. Here in France we drive on the right. Visitors to my country sometimes have accidents."

Jeremy sighed. He could understand that. He'd driven in Europe a number of times and never had a problem. His daughter would be driving overseas for the first time.

"Perhaps now I could look at the photos of your daughter?"

Jeremy opened an attaché case and withdrew an envelope. He removed several photographs and passed them to Emmanuel.

"Your daughter…she is very attractive," he observed.

"Is that important?"

"That is twice you have asked that question, Monsieur. You must understand, I cannot know what is important until it becomes so."

Jeremy held his impatience in check and nodded. "Of course. I understand and I apologise."

Emmanuel nodded and continued.

"Did your daughter indicate what she intended to visit during her visit to France … other than Paris, of course?"

"No, at least not in any detail. The usual tourist attractions … the Eiffel Tower, the Louvre Museum, Norte Dame Cathedral, the Arc de Triomphe and so on. Nowhere unusual. Certainly nothing surprising or risky."

"And you could track her on your phone?"

"I could. I used the Family Link app on our phones ... until I couldn't."

Emmanuel raised his eyebrows questioningly.

"I lost contact with her. It was on the fourth day. Her location didn't appear on the app. She didn't reply to messages. She didn't answer calls. That's when my concern for her safety began in earnest."

"Does your daughter have any favourite foods?" Jeremy frowned and Emmanuel smiled.

"If I know she enjoyed Italian cuisine, for example, I could contact the owners of such restaurants. If she liked Greek food ..."

"Yes. I get the idea. I believe she sometimes visited an Indian restaurant close to home. She would meet up with several of her female friends for an evening out. They might catch a film and then go on from there."

"Does she speak French? I ask because she could have asked someone for directions. That person might recall her having difficulty with our language."

"She's no linguist but she studied French at school and passed her exams. I would imagine she had street maps and she had her phone, of course, so she could use that for directions."

"Are you sure she travelled to France by boat?"

"As I've already told you, she collected a hire car from the port."

"So you did."

"I would imagine she caught a train from St Pancras in London to Dover Priory and hopped on to a cross-channel ferry from there."

"Hopped?" Emmanuel looked puzzled.

"Boarded," Jeremy clarified.

"A final question, Monsieur. Why have you come to me for assistance in discovering the whereabouts of your daughter? Why not report the matter to the French authorities?"

"Do you think they would be interested in using

their resources to find a young lady missing in your country for only four days?"

"I doubt it, Monsieur Richards. I doubt it. I have contacts, however."

"Which is why I have come to your office."

"I do not always succeed in my work. Whether I succeed or not in your case makes no difference to my fee. Win or lose. Succeed or fail. I do not refund money. Is that clear? Do you understand?"

"And if I offered you half now, in advance, and the other half when you succeed ..."

"*If* I succeed, monsieur. There are no guarantees in my line of work. Succeed or fail ... I still put in the same effort, I still seek out the same sources ... you can understand that, *oui*?"

"I guess so."

"You guess so? Well, you guess correctly."

"Okay. Okay. I will put my trust in your agency and my daughter's safety in your hands. Would you give me a ballpark figure, please?"

"Ballpark. You think this is a game? Finding your daughter is a game? I do not play games, monsieur. I use my abilities, my contacts, my hunches. Usually, I am successful. Sometimes, I am not. Whatever the outcome, I put in the same number of hours, the same amount of work, the same effort. *Comprenez-vous?*"

"The cost, please?"

"For acting solely on your case, I request a fee of €760 for an eight-hour day of my time."

"And how many days ...?"

Emmanuel shrugged his shoulders.

"For as many days or hours as you engage me to act on your behalf."

"And when do you decide that ... er..."

"Each day, I will share my findings with you and if, after three days, I have made no progress, I will return half of what you have paid me. You can then decide whether or not you wish me to continue acting on your behalf on the same terms."

"That's an awful lot of money," Jeremy mused.

"I cover an awful lot of ground during my enquiries."

"Payment in advance?"

"We can agree a contract that allows you to hire my services on a daily basis. The contract, I should add, is in compliance with articles 1984 to 2010 of the French Civil Code."

Jeremy said nothing for several long seconds before sharing his decision.

"I will pay you for three full days. After that, we can discuss any progress that has been made and take matters from there."

"As you wish, monsieur. I can start work on your case once I've taken down as much information and as many details as you can provide."

"And payment?"

"I shall have my secretary draw up the contract. It will be ready at eight tomorrow morning. You read it. You sign it. You pay me. I begin."

THREE

Jeremy entered the lift at a couple of minutes to eight the next morning. The corridors already echoed with footsteps and the opening and closing of doors. Maybe the staff made an early start in order to finish their day sooner and beat the rush-hour traffic jams.

He made his way to Monsieur Degarmo's office and knocked on the door. The private investigator could have been waiting behind the door – it opened a few seconds later and Jeremy was ushered into the office.

Degarmo wasted no time.

"The contract has been prepared. I will leave you for a short time while you read and agree it. If all is as you expect, kindly add your signature above mine on the final page."

"When would you like me to pay your fee?"

"I would be much obliged if you would make a

payment in advance of €2280 to cover the first three days. If, by some stroke of good fortune, I conclude your case sooner, you will be refunded the appropriate amount."

Jeremy drew a deep breath.

"If you can find her it will be worth every penny ... or Euro, I should say."

"Please listen carefully to the questions I am about to ask you. If you know the answers to any of them it could prove valuable."

Jeremy nodded and took a sip of water from the glass Degarmo's secretary had placed on a small table beside him.

"Your daughter's full name, monsieur?"

"Annabelle Louise Roberts."

"Her place and date of birth?"

"Cambridge. June 21st 2002."

"And a British citizen, I would imagine?"

"Cambridge, England. Yes, she's a British Citizen."

"Do you, perhaps, have any details from her passport ... the nine-digit passport code, the date it was issued, the expiry date?"

"I'm afraid not."

"You have shown me photos of your daughter. Is her appearance as presented or might it have changed?"

"I have no reason to think that."

"And do you have a copy of her signature, monsieur?"

Jeremy hesitated.

"Let me think. Yes ... at least of her first name. I have a letter from her telling me of her planned visit to France."

He withdrew an envelope from the inside pocket of his jacket, handed it to the detective and waited while he made a photocopy.

Once Degarmo had returned to his seat behind the desk, the questions continued.

"Merci. Please ... are you able to tell me the last

place, the date and time that anybody might have seen or had contact with Annabelle?"

"Well, no ... the people at the car hire depot, perhaps?"

"Oui. That is good. She was travelling alone?"

"Yes."

"Your daughter had a mobile phone, oui?"

"Yes. I have the mobile number."

"Do you know the make, the model, it's serial number?"

"I know it's a newish iPhone. She bought it on Amazon not long ago with money I gave her towards a birthday present."

"But I doubt you have the IMEI number of the phone?"

Jeremy looked puzzled.

The detective smiled. "It is the serial number of the phone. It can be helpful but does anyone ever know their phone's serial number?"

Jeremy shook his head.

But you have an email address?"

"Yes."

"Social media accounts?"

"I know she had friends on Facebook. I'm not aware of any others."

"Merci. I will make a note of the mobile number

and her email address. Can you provide that information?"

The detective pushed a sheet of blank paper and a biro towards Jeremy.

"I've no desire to hassle you but when do you think you might be able to start your investigation?"

"Monsieur ... I have already begun. After you left my office yesterday I informed the Paris Police Prefecture. It takes upon itself law enforcement duties within the city limits ... which is the obvious place to start the search. You agree?"

Jeremy nodded.

"I must say, you don't waste much time."

"Time is money, monsieur. *My* time and *your* money!"

FOUR

Emmanuel Degarmo studied the list he had been preparing. It was not complete but then how could it be? At the top he had written Eifel Tower and beneath this had added Louvre Museum and Notre Dame. Most visitors exploring Paris would visit these sites and he knew many of the assistants and guides that were employed at them. From there, he would criss-cross Paris and leave copies of the photos that Jeremy had provided of his daughter. This had proved fruitful on several occasions in the past but with so many visitors to the attractions of his city it would be a difficult task for his contacts to identify one amongst their number.

He would cast his net more widely later in the day and, time permitting, speak to friends in the Paris police who, in turn, might be prepared to spread their net more widely and seek help from the gendarmerie.

Jeremy had indicated his daughter's interest in history so tomorrow he would distribute photographs amongst the custodians of appropriate establishments. Jeremy had agreed to meet Emmanuel back at his office at five that afternoon so that the private investigator could update him on the day's activities.

Before that, however, there was somebody else he had to check on. He hailed a taxi and told its driver to take him to an address off the Rue du Volga. The traffic was growing heavy, being the tail-end of the working day, but there should be time enough if he kept the meeting brief. He glanced at his phone and pressed a couple of buttons. And there it was! His daughter's location. She hadn't moved away for at least an hour,

He knew more about his daughter's phone than he had led Emmanuel to believe. She had a favourite small backpack that she hardly ever left behind when out of doors. Sewn into its bottom lining was an air tag. He had put it there on an earlier occasion when she had paid him a visit on his birthday. As the taxi drew close to its destination, Jeremy opened 'Find my' on his i-phone and pressed the entry for 'Annabelle' … and there she was on Rue de Thorigny. She loved art and the work of Pablo Picasso. He and she had very different tastes and his opinion of the man's work was at odds with his daughter's. Not that it mattered. What did matter was knowing where she was but Emmanuel not knowing that he knew.

FIVE

Jeremy knocked on the investigator's door.

"*Entrez.*"

Emmanuel wasted no time.

"Your daughter visited The Musée Picasso-Paris Gallery this afternoon. She is still there. However, the gallery closes very shortly so she will have left before you could reach her."

Jeremy was astonished by Emmanuel's discovery. "How on earth ..." he began but then realised that the private detective had contacts across Paris. What puzzled him though was why he himself had been unable to find his daughter at the location displayed on his phone.

"Tomorrow, I shall follow-up more leads," the private detective said. "For now ... I would suggest you get some sleep and not to worry. I shall deliver her to you quite soon, I hope."

Jeremy shuddered at the word 'deliver' but thanked Emmanuel before leaving the office.

Once outside, he opened his phone and tapped out an encrypted message to his manager at Vauxhall Cross, London, headquarters of MI6's Secret Intelligence Service.

SIX

Once Jeremy had closed the door, Emmanuel stood up, walked across the floor and opened it again. Stepping outside, he looked both ways along the corridor and, satisfied that the Englishman had left, returned to his desk and dialled a number on his retro- style telephone. After two rings it was picked up.

"Degarmo. You're talking to Pierre. What do you have for me?"

SEVEN

Jeremy made an early start the following morning. This time, he paid for a taxi ride to The Musée Picasso-Paris Gallery. He wanted to be there at 9.30 when it opened its doors to the public. There were now three things he needed to find ... his daughter, her phone and her backpack. Actually, there was something else. How had the detective known Annabelle's location when he himself had failed to find her at the art gallery? He'd arrived just as it was on the point of closing and went directly to an information desk.

He'd approached an elderly assistant, showed him a photo of his daughter, and asked if he could remember having seen her, probably late afternoon the previous day. The man had shrugged his shoulders, rolled his eyes and swept his hand across an army of visitors milling around the entrance hall. He had a point.

Jeremy then spotted a young, female attendant standing just inside the entrance to the gallery and approached her.

"*Ma fille*," he began. "she visited the gallery yesterday afternoon but left without her backpack containing her mobile phone. Do you know if she has returned to collect it?"

"Un instant, monsieur."

The attendant walked away, presumably to a lost property office, and returned several minutes later.

"Je suis désolée, monsieur. Mais, non."

Jeremy thanked her for looking and then took the stairs to Le Café Sur Le Toit, the rooftop café within the museum. Over coffee and an éclair, he pondered what he should try next.

EIGHT

In his office, Emmanuel Degarmo walked over to a large cupboard and retrieved Annabelle's backpack. He checked that it still contained her phone and her passport but then why wouldn't it?

Only he and the young female attendant at the Gallery knew he had retrieved it from the 'lost items' room and she had been adequately rewarded in return for her silence and it would be foolish indeed for her to break her word.

NINE

Annabelle had just finished her meal when a man had approached her table and asked if she was Annabelle Roberts. He said her father was in Paris on business and had something important to tell her. He had a key meeting to attend, knew where she could be found, and had sent him to the museum to collect her. There was an important matter he needed to discuss with her before he returned to London.

"What important matter?" she had asked.

"*Me regrette ... je ne sais pas.*"

She picked up her rucksack and followed the man down a flight of stairs to the ground floor. They walked out of the museum and the man pointed towards a grey Citroen parked about twenty paces away.

Its engine was idling and, as they drew close, Annabelle made out a woman in dark glasses seated behind the steering wheel.

The man opened a rear door and indicated that Annabelle be seated. He then climbed into the passenger seat beside the woman and they drove through busy Paris suburbs for the best part of thirty minutes before pulling up outside a nondescript row of three houses separated by high hedges. Tall trees in front of the properties protected the privacy of their from the inquisitive eyes of any passers-by.

Annabelle began to feel uncomfortable. She had weighed common sense against not wishing to disappoint her father but had she got the balance right?

"Follow me," the man said. He began walking along a path that led to the front door of one of the three houses. Annabelle hesitated. She still had time to turn and walk away … or run if necessary. The woman in sunglasses prodded her forward.

"*Se dépêcher*," she said. "Hurry up."

Annabelle's heartbeat quickened. This didn't feel right. She turned around, took three quick steps back to the door and pulled down hard on the handle. The door didn't open.

"I'm sorry, mademoiselle," the woman said. Annabelle turned around. The woman was still wearing sunglasses but now she was also holding a wooden mallet in her right hand. Mesmerised by what she saw, Annabelle's heart skipped a beat and her eyes opened wide in disbelief as the woman swung her arm towards Annabelle's head.

TEN

Jeremy phoned his manager at Vauxhall Cross,

London.

"There's no sign of her or her backpack at the Picasso Museum. I've enquired but nobody I've spoken to recalls seeing her and her backpack has not been handed in to the Lost Property Office. I've phoned Emmanuel Degarmo and he assures me that no taxi service is aware of picking her up in Paris but he remains confident of finding her."

"You still trust him?" the man from MI6 asked.

"His references are impeccable," Jeremy replied.

"Well, I'm sure they would be. You really should have approached me first before taking matters into your own hands."

"Going through the proper channels would have

been time-consuming and I was worried for my daughter's safety. The authorities here do not accept a missing person report until a certain amount of time has passed and Degarmo comes with impeccable references."

"Update me tomorrow," his manager said curtly and hung up.

ELEVEN

Annabelle opened her eyes and thought she must be in Hell. She found herself in total darkness. There was no light. Her head was throbbing. She dare not move. Had she died and been transported to a dark underworld? Surely not. She could think and she could reason, at least to an extent … but where was she? What had happened? Her thoughts were irrational and her reasoning illogical. She shivered.

In a crazy way she felt surrounded by Death. Her stomach churned but not simply from fear. She was hungry. It felt as though she hadn't eaten for days but knew that couldn't be so. There was still a slight taste in her mouth of the grilled cheese panini she had eaten in the Picasso Gallery.

The more she became aware of her situation the greater her fear increased. Her eyes were slowly adjusting to the darkness but instead of it making matters slightly better it made them infinitely worse!

She struggled to understand what had happened to land her in this dark and ominous place although her memory was slowly moving into gear. The Picasso Museum … the man approaching her in the cafeteria on the first floor. He said he would take her to her father. There was a car waiting outside and a woman in sunglasses in the driver's seat. She was driven to a house screened from the street and … there had been excruciating pain … like a hammer blow to her head …and then nothing… until now.

From her position, propped up against a wall, there was little to see at first but as her eyes adjusted to her surroundings, she cast her gaze around her new surroundings. The vast space felt dark and menacing but it wasn't until her eyes began to focus that she began screaming.

TWELVE

Jeremy tapped his fingers impatiently on the desk.

"So you've made no progress?"

Emmanuel Degarmo smiled. "It is … how do you say …early days, monsieur. I have made progress. I have been in touch with several of my best contacts. I do not know where she is but I know where she isn't. That, monsieur, is progress."

"I suppose I should tell you that I visited The Musée Picasso-Paris Gallery yesterday. We both know she went there but the staff I spoke to had no recollection of seeing either her or her rucksack."

"Monsieur, so perhaps you should leave me to do the … how do you say … donkey work?"

"Of course … but it does no harm to feed the donkey."

THIRTEEN

Jeremy felt compelled to return to his daughter's last known sighting so after leaving Degarmo's office he hailed a taxi and returned to the Picasso Museum.

The Museum was less busy than he remembered it that morning and Jeremy passed few people as he climbed the stairs to the cafeteria on the first floor. It was empty apart from a young couple sitting with coffees and croissants at a corner table.

A young woman behind the counter smiled as he approached. "*Oui, Monsieur?*"

He felt a little guilty not ordering food or drink.

"Please … I'm trying to find my daughter. She visited the museum just a couple of days ago. Here … I have a photo." He opened his phone and thumbed his way to several photos of her. "You recognise her?"

"Mais, oui."

"Was she on her own?"

"*Oui* … but a man approached her and they left together a few minutes later."

"Forgive me but could you describe him?

The young woman smiled as she said,

"Smartly dressed … and *il avait un petit moustache.*"

FOURTEEN

Annabelle could dimly make out a tall shape against a wall to one side of her. The shape was irregular, with ragged edges and sloping sides that formed an untidy pyramid. She rose unsteadily to her feet. Her head felt as if it had been used to hammer home nails and it took several painful moments before she was finally upright.

She took five steps towards the pyramid. It would have been further but her body had frozen. She stared at the sight that met her eyes and it stared back at her! A thousand empty sockets, where once there had been eyes, were staring vacantly at her. They stared from above her, below her and from every angle imaginable ... empty human skulls with gaping mouths and stubs of teeth. They were stacked perhaps twenty or more high with hundreds of bare white bones poking out from above, beneath, between and on all sides of them.

Annabelle screamed and passed out.

*

FIFTEEN

Early next morning, Jeremy left the apartment he was renting and took a cab to Avenue Marceau and entered the building with its long corridors, winding staircases and numerous offices. He opted for the lift on this occasion. It would be quicker and leave him with sufficient breath for what he had to say.

He rapped twice on the door bearing the black letters ED. There was no response so he tried again. Still nothing. He turned the door's handle and pushed against it. It didn't open.

At that moment he heard footsteps echo in one of the corridors and prepared himself for a confrontation but the figure that rounded the corner was not that of Emmanuel. It was another male but this one was carrying a small tool bag. He stopped when he reached Emmanuel's door and reached into the bag.

"Monsieur Degarmo is not in his office," La he told the man in French.

The man simply shrugged and reached into his bag for a screwdriver … and then removed the two screws securing the plate with the initials ED to the door.

SIXTEEN

Jeremy found a quiet alcove within the building and extracted his phone. Within fifteen seconds he was speaking to his manager at Vauxhall Cross.

"So now we have two missing persons?"

"Two?"

"Your daughter and your wonderful private investigator."

Jeremy held his tongue. If there ever was a time to get angry with his superior this was not it. Several worrying seconds passed. He could almost hear his boss sighing deeply.

"Don't wander too far from your apartment. I'll see what I can find out."

Jeremy was on the point of saying 'thank you, sir'

but the call to his manager had been disconnected.

SEVENTEEN

He had hardly caught his breath before his phone played its merry announcement of an incoming call.

"Surprised to hear from me, Monsieur Richards?"

"Degarmo! What have you done with my daughter?"

"Your daughter is perfectly safe … certainly for the moment."

"What the hell is that supposed to mean?"

"As I just told you. For the moment."

"If you've laid a finger on her … if you've hurt her in any way …"

"Your daughter is quite safe and as well as can be expected … in the circumstances."

"What circumstances? What have you done to her?"

"Nothing that cannot be resolved with a few euros."

"You want money? Have I not paid what you asked?"

"*Certainement*, Monsieur … but I want more."

"More? What the hell are you talking about? How much more?"

"Two million more … but don't be alarmed. I'm talking euros not pounds."

EIGHTEEN

Annabelle screamed. Closed her eyes. Opened them and screamed again. She realised that this was not some nightmare from within a troubled night's sleep. This was real.

She was surrounded by skulls. Not a few, not a dozen but hundreds upon hundreds piled high all around her.

She turned around. There was a flight of well-worn stone steps about fifty metres from her. Or was she imagining it? Was she hallucinating? She tried to stand but her legs were weak from cramp and she sank back down onto the stone floor.

"Hello?" She'd have died of fright if there had been a reply from one of the skulls.

Annabelle rose painfully to her knees and forced herself upright. It took several moments for her to gain sufficient strength in her legs to shuffle across the floor towards the steps. There must have been a hundred or more. She gingerly placed a foot on the first step and slipped, only just managing to remain upright.

She thought there was the faintest glimmer of light at the base of the door above her but the steps were far too wet and slippery to contemplate an attempt to reach it. What would she find on the other side of that door? Somewhere above her was the world of the living. Down here in the corridors of bones and skulls lived the dead.

NINETEEN

Degarmo felt smug. This was the most profitable case he had ever been involved in. The path he had taken to obtain such a fortune was not one to be lauded but as soon as two million euros were left beside the door of the address he had given Jeremy this affair would be over.

TWENTY

Jeremy's phone played its tune and he picked up.

"Do as he asks. I have arranged for the money to

be deposited into the French BNP Paribas. The branch address is 8 Rue de Sofia, 75018 Paris. I've opened an account in your name."

"You're not worried that I might open an account in my own name, withdraw the money … and disappear?"

"I hope that's a poor joke, Jeremy. You could run but you could never hide."

"You're right, of course. I don't want to hide, I just want to find my daughter."

"There's a branch not too far from you. I'll message you its address. Take a cab. You'll be reimbursed the fare."

"That's generous of you."

"Generous? Hardly. I want fifty per cent of the ransom money."

"You want what?"

"Joking, old man, only joking."

"Do you happen to have an address for the bank, sir?"

"What? Some detective you're turning out to be, Jeremy."

"Okay, okay. I'll find it."

"I have every confidence in you. Tell me once you've withdrawn the money and I'll tell you where I've arranged for the exchange to take place. Oh … and good luck."

TWENTY ONE

The bank was situated at 39 Rue Croix des Petits Champs, 75001 in Paris.

Withdrawing such an enormous sum of money proved incredibly easy. After dealing with the paperwork, the bank manager asked that he leave quietly through a side door situated at the rear of the building. His deputy would follow after a few minutes with a small suitcase containing the money.

The exchange duly took place and was completed with a firm handshake. It was all so ridiculously simple! Jeremy now needed to find out where he was to take the small fortune he was holding.

TWENTY TWO

Annabelle was surprised at how soon she was able to view her surroundings without feeling she would be physically sick. Bones, bones, bones. Bones and skulls, and ribs … she shuddered but took a few tentative steps along a damp, soft track wound through an arch that was twice her height. Beside it she could see another arch and then another. The path wound itself through the arches like a long, frenzied snake seeking escape from this tunnel of death.

She pushed a button on the side of her smart watch and the screen became illuminated. As far as she could judge, she had taken three hundred steps and travelled about a tenth of a mile but had no way of knowing if the meandering path was leading her round in circles or leading to a setting more shocking than the one in which she was already entrapped.

TWENTY THREE

"I have the money."

Jeremy had answered another call from Degarmo.

"I know you do. I was watching. I'm a private detective, monsieur. I watched you go to the bank. More importantly, I saw you come out with the suitcase, which I thought most generous of its staff. Now ... no more banter, Jeremy. Go to this address ... 21 bis, Avenue René-Coty. You will find a wooden door. It will be locked, Do not try to pick the lock or force it open in any way. Is that clear?" knew I could rely on you to see sense, Monsieur Roberts. Now, do you have a pen? I'm going to give you an address."

"Hold on."

Jeremy put down the caseload of money he was carrying and ferreted in his jacket pocket for a pen.

"You'll never get away with this," he said as he tore a sheet of paper from the notebook that he always made a point of carrying with him.

"Oh, I think I will, Jeremy old boy. This is the address you are to go to. Make sure you write it down correctly. I don't want to waste my time."

"Okay. Give me the address."

"*21 bis, Avenue René-Coty.*"

"That is good. Please read back to me the address I have just given you."

"Is that really necessary?"

"You wish to have back your daughter? Do it!"

"*21 bis, Avenue René-Coty.*"

"Good. Leave the suitcase behind the recycling bins that have been placed there and then walk away. Continue walking along the Avenue for ten minutes."

"And my daughter?"

"She will be outside the door waiting for you ...

but only if you do exactly as I say. *Comprenez-vous?*"

"Perfectly."

"Good. I will collect the money and have your daughter waiting for you once I am assured you have followed my instructions. You and Annabelle, will soon be reunited."

TWENTY FOUR

Annabelle shivered. Being scared to death had become more than a metaphor. Although she shivered, the temperature displayed on her smartwatch suggested it was 14 degrees. She was hungry, tired and thirsty and growing wearier and more despairing by the minute. Surely the path she was on must soon lead to a way out of this ghastly mausoleum of bones.

TWENTY FIVE

Few people are beyond temptation where money is concerned. The poor need it but the rich become greedy and want more than they could ever need whilst those in genuine need might steal a loaf of bread from a boulangerie and find themselves before a magistrate appointed by the President of France. Life was far from fair for some.

TWENTY SIX

Monsieur Maurice Garnier was the bank manager of the bank and Pierre Picard was the deputy that had courteously carried the suitcase of money out to Jeremy.

However, what nobody was aware of, apart from themselves, of course, was that a tracking device had been placed amongst the bank notes. They knew where to find two million euros.

TWENTY SEVEN

Jeremy thought his heartbeat must be heard across the whole of Paris … all the way from Avenue du Colonel Henri Rol-Tanguy to Rue Croix des Petits Champs. He had the money and he had a destination. What he did not have … yet … was his daughter. When did she first go missing? Would she be alive, and well, and waiting for him when he reached Avenue du Colonel Henri Rol-Tanguy, the address Degarmo had given him?

TWENTY EIGHT

The tour guide raises his arm and the group of ten tourists fall silent and turn towards him … apart from one, that is, who seems more interested in a set of refuse bins situated about five metres from the entrance door to the catacombs.

"Excuse me, sir, but are you with my party?" he asks in French.

"*Mais, non*," the man replies. "I'm just looking for something I may have dropped earlier."

"Perhaps we could help you find it. The

Catacombs don't open for another fifteen minutes."

A suitcase containing two million euros?

"It's very kind of you but it's nothing important."
... but if you find a terrified and hungry young woman amongst the ossuaries please inform her that she will soon be reunited with her father.

Jeremy watched events unfold from a seat in the corner of a café. He had no set plan but he did have a camera on his phone and he used it now to film Degarmo. He wanted clear proof that the man had picked up the suitcase of money and then ask his manager back in London to inform the French police. There was more than just money at stake ... there was the recovery of his daughter.

TWENTY NINE

"The Catacombs of Paris form an underground ossuary that holds the remains of more than six million people. They extend south from the Barrière d'Enfer which was once the city gate."

"Somebody had a wretched job digging such an enormous hole in the ground," a young man remarked. "I bet they had backache!"

"Not so, The ossuary was located in old limestone quarries and was used to hold the remains of six million Parisians. Originally, it was a place for storing bones from cemeteries that no longer had sufficient space of their own.

In 1809, Inspector Héricart de Thury was appointed general inspector of quarries, a position he held for over twenty years. During that time, he researched and consolidated the former subterranean mines of Paris of which The Catacombs of Paris is the most famous.

Shortly, we shall enter the catacomb and you will discover for yourself how he transformed it into a unique and visually striking display. Héricart de Thury arranged the bones into various patterns and shapes."

Degarmo stood aside as the group of tourists began descending the one hundred and thirty one steps into the heart of the ossuary where Héricart de Thury had decorated and arranged the bones into various patterns and designs.

"If time permits, you should also visit the 'Z' Room which is actually situated directly below the École Normale Supérieure which showcases Romanesque-style vaults."

Degarmo edged his way past the tourists. Maybe he had made a bad decision. He did not expect Annabelle to be discovered ... at least, not alive. That wouldn't do. She was a loose end and loose ends night wrap themselves around somebody's neck ... namely his own. If he was to enjoy the contents of the suitcase that Jeremy had tucked away out of sight then a loose end around his neck was quite unacceptable. The thought made him smile. But he had to be sure about the girl. How far into the catacombs could she have travelled? He had noted the footprints imbedded in the damp pathway that stretched from the bottom of the one hundred and thirty one steps before winding through the arches and mounds of skeletal remains that lined the corridors of bones. How far could the young woman have travelled? The hammer blow to her head had been well placed and when he had unlocked the entrance door to the crypt and pushed her down the steps he assumed she would die from internal bleeding. So where was the wretched girl?

The tourists were either enthralled or horrified by

the sight of thousand upon thousand bones and skulls stacked neatly as exhibits. It was almost as refined as the works on display at the Musee National Picasso-Paris.

The tour guide had dragged his listeners closer to Degarmo.

"We will soon be approaching the 'Z' Room. One interesting fact worth noting is that it is situated directly below the École Normale Supérieure which is considered one of the leading higher education institutions in Paris and is well-regarded internationally."

"You wouldn't catch me reading schoolbooks if I knew I was standing on the heads of all these dead people."

I don't think I'd catch you reading any books, the guide thought to himself.

THIRTY

The catacomb circuit measures one and a half kilometres and Degarmo had been amongst the bones for twenty minutes. Allowing for any delay caused by the dawdling touring group he reckoned he was at least halfway around and still there was no sign of Annabelle. Where the hell was she?

THIRTY ONE

Jeremy was growing impatient. He was on his

third cup of dark-roasted French coffee and still there was no sign of Degarmo, his daughter or of someone removing the case-load of money that would transform their life.

The café owner appeared in the doorway and then moved round the outdoor tables unnecessarily wiping their surfaces. Perhaps he thought Jeremy should buy some food from him if he intended spending all day simply sitting and staring at passers-by.

Jeremy stood up. Maybe it was time to move off. He was tempted to establish that the suitcase was still there behind the large recycling bins but the café owner was watching him and might wonder what he was up to.

THIRTY TWO

Claude was well known on the pavements around the catacombs of Paris. They were home to him most nights and on wet and windy days shop doorways provided him with some shelter but little comfort. Beggars were rife in the capital city and Claude was one of their number. He had scrawled on a large piece of cardboard torn from a box that he'd found in a discarded shopping trolley.

'Pour mangers s'il vous plait'. For food, please. For food … he needed money. He had none. He relied on the kindness and sympathy of passers-by. Either that or he go scavenging … which he was about to do.

He struggled to his feet from the stone-hard pavement and shuffled towards the recycling bins that were about ten metres from the entrance to the Paris catacombs. They always looked clean and tidy. They were certainly no eyesore. Sometimes, but not often, he would see something useful that had been discarded. He lifted the lids of all three bins … but not today. However, there was a small gap between the 'paper' and 'plastic' bins and something caught his eye. He could see what he thought to be a small, black suitcase. The gap was too small for him to squeeze between. He tried moving one of the bins but it was too heavy. The same with the second. The third must have been empty and he was able to wriggle it towards him until there was a gap sufficient that he could reach through with his arm to the suitcase. He could now touch it but how was he to pull it towards him?

He waited … after several minutes a muscular young man stopped by the bins to light a cigarette and Claude approached him.

"Please, monsieur … there is a small suitcase behind this bin. It would be so useful for carrying food and my few belongings but the bin is too heavy to move on my own."

"Not a problem, Claude." So the young man recognised him! So much the better, he surmised.

The man wriggled and tugged the bin until he

was able to reach through with his arm and lift it up and over onto the pavement. Not only that but he took a ten-euro note from his pocket.

"Buy yourself some food," he said.

Claude watched him walk away and then picked up the suitcase and carried it into the Parc Montsouris.

THIRTY THREE

Subdued lighting must have been switched on because the path was now more visible. Even so, Annabelle heard somebody curse as they stumbled on a skull that had rolled from a stack of bones onto the track. She ducked behind a pillar and held her breath.

Moments later, a figure passed within two metres of her. And then he called out her name!

"Annabelle! Mon dieu! Where the devil are you? Can you hear me? Your father is waiting for you at the exit. I can lead you to him."

Annabelle held her breath. She recognised the voice. She knew who was calling to her. It was the man that had tricked her into leaving the café over the Musée Picasso.

"You don't know the way out of here, you silly girl! There are almost a quarter of a million metres of bone-encrusted tunnels under Paris. You need my help if you hope to ever to find your way out of here."

THIRTY FOUR

Pierre was close to one of his favourite places in Paris. Parc Montsouris, with its sweeping lawns, trees, small bridges and picturesque grottoes, offered him shelter when it rained, shade during a hot summer and, right now, a bench to himself in a quiet spot beside a picturesque miniature waterfall. The suitcase was locked but he knew it was one he could force open. But what would he find? Warm clothes for the next winter? Clean socks and underwear? Sweet-smelling deodorants to cover an unwashed body and bring benefactors closer? He withdrew a biro pen from a trouser pocket and forced it into the suitcase's zip. Thirty seconds later, he had the case open.

THIRTY FIVE

Annabelle could hear people chattering. Their voices grew louder as they drew closer to where she was hiding from Degarmo. Degarmo, meanwhile, was debating with himself whether to give up his search for Jeremy's daughter and simply go directly to the exit door on Avenue du Colonel Henri Rol-Tanguy and recover the suitcase of money from behind the recycling bins. However, if Annabelle was still alive and had somehow managed to exit the catacombs, she would have alerted the authorities or have asked to use somebody's phone to contact her father. Either way, by then he would be out of the country. He had his passport with him, could flag down a cab to take him to Charles de Gaulle airport and arrive in England in time for dinner at the Ritz.

THIRTY SIX

Claude looked around to reassure himself that he was unobserved as he opened the suitcase. A clean, white shirt might serve him well when begging and clean socks and underwear would mean not having to use hand basins in public toilets. Some warm clothing for next winter? A handkerchief, perhaps, to wipe his fingerprints from the suitcase if its owner had not, in fact, dumped and discarded it behind the bins but had hidden it out of sight with the intention of retrieving it later.

THIRTY SEVEN

The tourist group grew level with the heavy pillar that shielded Annabelle. She grasped the opportunity to attach herself to the back of them and slowly work her way in amongst them. Nobody seemed to notice albeit their number was quite small.

However, *Degarmo* noticed a trail of footprints on the dusty ground leading from the nearby support column that he hadn't previously noticed ... which irritated him because he was supposed to notice such things. He was a very good private detective!

And then he finally spotted her. She hadn't found

a way out of the catacombs on her own after all and nor had she died from the hammer blow to her head. At least, not yet.

She was with a group of tourists, almost hidden amongst them. He needed to get her on her own before it was too late. She would be his bargaining chip if the suitcase of money was not behind the recycling bins as Jeremy had agreed.

Meanwhile ... messieurs Maurice Garnier and Pierre Picard paid the taxi driver who had dropped them off a couple of hundred metres from the exit of the catacombs at 21 bis, Avenue René-Coty. There was no sign of Jeremy which could mean one of three things. Either he had not kept his word, kept the money for himself and disappeared with it ... or the two million euros were, indeed, still nestled in the suitcase and would very shortly fall into their laps ...

...which is almost exactly what happened when Claude finally prised open into the suitcase except that the bank notes didn't fall into his lap but on to the grass around where he was sitting ... and where a sudden gust of summer wind sent them scurrying across the grass. He lowered the lid but couldn't secure it because he had damaged the zip when forcing it open. Parc Montsouris was growing busy. People were travelling home from work and began queuing at the sunken Cité Universitaire train stop created by Alphonse Alphand. The RER train cuts right through the park along a sunken trackway lined with pine trees. Children were being taken to the park's playgrounds or gathering at the puppet theatre for a late afternoon performance.

A warm wind swept over the suitcase and wafted the bank notes across the grass and flower beds. Passers-by scurried after them. Claude closed the lid and pulled one end of the seat down on to the top of the case to protect the rest of the banknotes. Now he was faced with a dilemma. Should he, too, chase after the money and leave the case unattended, or drag it by its handle somewhere secluded. There was nowhere obvious to hide it. Could he wedge it below the bench and leave it unattended for fifteen minutes whilst he trotted off to collect plastic shopping bags from a supermarket? Or would it be quicker to return to the recycling bins and see if there were any discarded bags inside them?

THIRTY EIGHT

Emmanuel had no difficulty exiting the catacombs. Everybody in Paris knew where they began and where they finished. No doubt, some of them had found permanent accommodation in them. He lingered at the back of the group, shielded himself from Annabelle, should she turn around, and walked away from the tourists. After about fifty metres he looked back over his shoulder. The guide and his party were out of sight ... but then so was Annabelle.

THIRTY NINE

Maurice Garnier checked his iPhone. He was getting a strong signal and his Find My app pinpointed the location of the suitcase containing the money that he and Pierre Picard intended spending on new and lavish lifestyles. Garnier even harboured thoughts of one day writing a book about what they had achieved.

FORTY

Annabelle could make herself understood in French albeit she was not particularly au fait with the language. However, she desperately needed to contact her father. He never said very much about what his work entailed but she knew he worked as an agent for MI6 in London … and now she needed to find a police officer who could make sense of her halting knowledge of his language and take her seriously when she asked for help finding her father. She needed to expose Degarmo for what he really was … a violent and dangerous rogue … and that was putting it mildly.

Within ten minutes she caught sight of two police cars parked by the side of the road opposite Parc Montsouris. A gendarme was standing beside one of the cars. He had a walkie-talkie in one hand and a fistful of 500 euro notes in the other. Just one of those would cover the cost of my trip to Paris, she thought. She approached him.

"Excusez-moi. Je recherche mon père."

"You have lost your father?" he asked in English.

"*Oui*. I mean, 'yes'."

He crossed to the other side of his car and opened the door. "S'asseoir, s'il vous plaît." Sit down, please.

FORTY ONE

Claude didn't know whether to laugh or to cry. The paper money fluttered in the breeze like snow and park users were scurrying about like bees in a hive as they chased after it. He had hoped for a clean, white shirt but he now had enough money stuffed into his pockets to buy a hundred … a thousand … not to mention a mug of tea and a crusty baguette.

A gendarme was trying frantically to stop the frenzied activity but he had a futile task on his hands.

FORTY TWO

Maurice Garnier stood beside the recycling bins that were close to the exit door of the Paris Catacombs with a look of disbelief on his face. He turned to face his bank deputy, Pierre Picard.

"I do not understand this. When I checked the tracking device a half hour ago, it put the suitcase here."

"How accurate is it?" Pierre Picard asked as he scoured the immediate vicinity.

"Very accurate. We are in the open. The sky is

clear. The signal is strong."

"Perhaps the clouds are blocking the signal," Pierre suggested.

"They shouldn't affect it but do that … take a look."

Pierre returned within twenty seconds.

"No. There's nothing there apart from a piece of cardboard with a few words scrawled across it."

"A few words? A clue, perhaps. What did it say?"

'Pour mangers s'il vous plait.'

FORTY THREE

Degarmo was frustrated and furious with himself.

He had lost his confidence, his dignity and his self-esteem though not necessarily in that order. Months of careful planning and finally grasping an unexpected opportunity to feather his nest with all that money could buy ... it was all slipping away from him.

He crossed the road to a quiet café and sat watching the cars and people pass by.

"*Monsieur?*" a waiter asked.

"*Un café noir, s'il vous plait,*" Degarmo replied.

A sudden gust of warm wind swept a small piece of paper into his face. He wiped it away and then caught his breath. It was more than simply a small piece of paper ... it was a five-hundred-euro bank note!

Degarmo looked up. Gusts of wind were swirling more notes over and around his head and people were chasing after them. This was crazy! He stood up, left some loose change on the table and grabbed the arm of one of those chasing the money.

"Where did this money come from?"

"My friend … the answer is blowing in the wind! Go to Le Parc Montsouris. It's raining five-hundred-euro notes!"

FORTY FOUR

The gendarme in the second of the two cars parked outside the park stirred when his radio crackled into life.

"There are reports of bank notes being blown around in Le Parc Montsouris. Probably nonsense but best take a look."

The second gendarme wore an amused expression as he entered the park ... but the smile faded when the breeze moulded a five-hundred-euro note to his nose.

Then he saw somebody he recognised crawling on hands and knees along the grass and pouncing on the dancing bank notes.

"Monsieur Degarmo!" he called out. "What on earth are you doing? Is business so bad that you turned from catching criminals to catching snails?"

"*Bon après-midi, monsieur.* Actually, all this money belongs to me."

The gendarme smiled and dropped a hand to his waist.

It was only when he heard a metallic clink that he glanced up …

… and when he did glance up he found himself looking not only at a gendarme dangling a pair of handcuffs from his hands but, in addition, he heard the siren start up on the second police vehicle and watched it accelerate away from the park and into the stream of early evening traffic.

FORTY FIVE

Maurice Garnier and Pierre Picard began to panic. They had witnessed the activity in and around the park as they had drifted away from the rear of the catacombs but it wasn't until they saw the two cars parked beside Parc Montsouris that a thought occurred to them ...

Maurice groaned.

"The police are looking for us," he muttered.

"Impossible!" Pierre exclaimed.

Maurice shook his head.

"No ... not impossible. They could have traced the source of the signal being sent to the tracking device we put in the suitcase."

"The source?" Pierre's complacency disappeared in an instant.

"I never thought to ask ... how does the device work? I've never used one."

"It sends a signal from its source to the device that we planted amongst the money in the suitcase."

"And where, exactly, is the source?"

"On the phone in my pocket!"

Pierre's heartbeat quickened.

"The two police cars outside the park ..."

Maurice completed the sentence.

"... have probably come for us!"

FORTY SIX

Degarmo was assisted back on to his feet by the gendarme and the pair began walking back to the police car that had remained parked by the side of the road outside Parc Montsouris. By this time, a small crowd had begun to gather bemused by this addition to their afternoon's entertainment.

Towards the back of them, however, were two men anything but amused.

"Pierre ... we need to return to those recycling bins."

"But the suitcase is no longer there ..."

"Maybe not ... perhaps it is ... but our fingerprints certainly are!"

The two men casually walked away from the small gathering. They were tempted to break into a run but they crossed the road at a normal pace to avoid drawing attention to themselves. They reached the bins and looked back.

More police had arrived and were talking to people from the crowd that had gathered.

"I think they're on to us," Pierre said shakily.

"Go round the back of the bins. We've got to hide!"

"*The bank manager and his deputy caught behind rubbish bins in famous park*. I can see tomorrow morning's headlines in Le Monde."

"Not if I can help it" Maurice retorted. "Quick ... into the bins!"

"What?"

"We have to hide. Climb into a bin!"

FORTY SEVEN

Jeremy was feeling exceedingly anxious. He was seated at the dining room table of the chambre d'hôte that he had booked for the duration of his stay in Paris. He had a copy of that morning's Le Monde in front of him and its front-page headline raised his heart-rate by several bpm.

'Bank managers rob their own bank! Police are searching for Maurice Garnier, the manager of BNP Paribas, on Rue Croix des Petits Champs, and his deputy, Pierre Picard. Both men are believed to have answers to the question ... where are the two million euros missing from the bank's vaults?'

It article went on to say that the previous afternoon it had been raining five-hundred-euro notes in Parc Montsouris.

FORTY EIGHT

"Can you hear me?" Pierre Picard called out. His voice echoed against the sides of the metal rubbish receptacle.

"Mon dieu! Keep your voice down! Better still, say nothing at all!"

Pierre almost immediately went against his bank manager's instruction.

"What is that noise?"

If his manager had bothered to reply, his words were inaudible above the rumble of a heavy vehicle.

The recycling lorry drew to a halt beside the bins and two men in overalls jumped down from either side of the vehicle's cabin.

"*Non! Non! Non!*"

The workmen looked at each other in

astonishment.

"*Qui êtes-vous?*" "Who are you?" one of them shouted.

"I am the manager of BNP Paribas" Maurice Garnier replied.

"Oui? And I am the President of the United States," the second worker responded.

"And I am his deputy," Pierre Picard added from the second refuse bin.

"Stay where you are until the shrink arrives to take you both back to the asylum."

"What? We're not mad!"

"Of course you're not. It's a warm day and you

were looking for some shade, no doubt"

Both workmen laughed, the driver started the engine, and they drove away.

FORTY NINE

Jeremy answered his phone. The call was from his boss at MI6 in London.

"Jeremy … I haven't heard from you lately. Do you mind telling me what's going on?"

"My apologies, sir, but things have turned a bit crazy over here."

"Crazy? What do you mean? Have you found your daughter?"

"Not yet …" His phone pinged.

"I'll call you back, sir."

Suddenly, everyone wanted to speak to him.

"Annabelle! Thank goodness. Where are you?"

"I'm not far from the Paris catacombs. Do you know them?"

"I know of them. I've never felt the urge to walk among the dead."

"Well, I've just escaped from thousands upon thousands of the bones that have been piled up and put on display."

"Why were you doing there? What on earth were you thinking of? I thought you were going to visit the Picasso Gallery."

"I was. I did …it's a long story but right now I'm trying to get as far as I can from people that are trying to kill me."

"What on earth do you mean?"

"It's a long story."

"Degarmo!"

"You know him?"

"He's a private detective. It's a long story. Just tell me where you are. I'll arrange for a taxi to collect you."

"Hang on a mo…I need to check where I am ... okay, so I'm on Rue de Rennes heading towards Notre Dame."

"Okay. Find somewhere to stand where you're easily seen. Say to the driver 'I'm Jeremy's daughter' and he'll bring you to me."

"But where are you?"

The phone went dead.

"Sorry, sir. That was my daughter. It's Degarmo ... he's leading me a merry dance."

"A merry dance, I should say, where every step has cost the department at least a thousand euros!"

FIFTY

Degarmo sat despondently in a holding cell.

Yesterday, he was about to become a man of vast

wealth. Today, he was being held by police awaiting an appearance in court, charged with abduction, attempted murder, deception and obtaining money by extortion. He had no illusions what tomorrow would bring. Life for him would continue but from behind the bars of a prison cell unless ...

FIFTY ONE

Annabelle watched the cars passing by. Several minutes passed and then one with a red 'TAXI' sign on its roof slowed as it approached her.

The driver wound down a window. He didn't bother to get out of his car.

"Annabelle Roberts?"

She opened a rear door and climbed in. The taxi sped away.

"*Où allons-nous?*" she asked. The driver pretended not to hear. She hoped her father knew what he was doing but hadn't the courage to ask the driver if she could borrow his phone.

After a short but traffic-heavy journey, the driver pulled up in front of an apartment block off the main thoroughfare. And there he was! Her father.

He took a couple of steps forward and hugged her.

"I've been so worried about you. I've wasn't able to contact you so I went to the Musee Picasso to ask if they recollected seeing you there …if was somewhere I felt sure you would visit … but drew a blank. I couldn't reach you by phone or email …"

"A man approached me in the café over the museum. He tricked me into going with him to a house. There was a woman – she drove the car. I was told you would be there. After we arrived, it soon became obvious you weren't there and then …"

Annabelle hesitated.

"Go on … and then what?"

"I don't know!"

"What do you mean, *you don't know*?"

"I must have been struck with something heavy and lost consciousness. When I came round, I found myself at the bottom of a flight of steps. It was quite dark and the steps were slippery and …"

Annabelle hesitated.

"And what?"

"Everywhere I looked there were … bones! Piles of them … and stacks of human skulls!"

"The Paris catacombs. They go back a long way. The churchyards in Paris ran out of space and the catacombs were built to house remains. They're not on every tourist's list of places to visit."

"I was terrified! I kept thinking that man was

going to return and add me to one of the heaps!"

FIFTY TWO

"I can help you recover much of the money," Emmanuel Degarmo told a senior officer at the police station where he was being held.

"Oh. And how would you manage to do that?"

"I am a private detective. It is my job to know such things. I understand the minds of villains."

"I don't doubt you have personal knowledge of such things, monsieur. Let's suppose I believe you. Let's suppose we do recover some of the two million euros ... what would you expect in return?"

"I would expect a stiff reprimand and a stern warning regarding my future conduct when working with clients."

The senior officer smiled.

"I will consider your request but tell me ... why did the money leave the bank in the first place?"

Ransom money ... Degarmo knew he was on to a loser regardless of his cooperation.

FIFTY THREE

French bank notes with a value of 500 euros have serial numbers that begin with the letter 'U'. If two or more have consecutive numbers they are likely to have been stolen. This would be how

Degarmo intended to begin his search for the missing money. Anybody with two such high-denomination notes, more especially with consecutive numbers fronted with a 'U' would become a focus of his pursuit. The trail began on the day Jeremy knocked on his office door and sought his services ... and continued after Jeremy was blackmailed into procuring two million Euros from his manager at MI6 ... and then collected the ransom money from the bank at 39 Rue Croix des Petits Champs, 75001.

FIFTY FOUR

The money had been packed into a suitcase generously provided by the bank ... and then, interestingly, after about fifteen minutes, Jeremy left the bank by a side door and hailed a taxi. Minutes later, Pierre Picard, the deputy manager, whom Degarmo recognised from his previous dealings with the bank, left by the same door apparently in pursuit ... and then Maurice Garnier, the bank's manager, had pulled out of the bank's car park and joined the queue. The motorcade then set out in pursuit of Jeremy and the money…

FIFTY FIVE

Claude probably had no need to beg ever again but old habits die hard.

He sat on the ground by the entrance to the park with the board propped up against the railings behind him.

'*Pour mangers s'il vous plait*'. For food, please.

It amused him to see that there were still people in the park, on their hand and knees, pushing aside bushes and ferreting in flower beds in search of a bank note that might earn them a cinema ticket and a good meal or a cross-channel trip to England. The two plastic carrier bags that he had taken from a supermarket were stuffed full of banknotes and in a cupboard at the back of his bedroom. The people of Paris were generous and he had long ago been able to rent an apartment within a thirty-minute walk from his begging patch. Perhaps he would replace his furniture and his bed and buy a larger television with his newly-found euros. Best to maintain his beggar's persona and allow time to pass before splashing out on luxuries. If one could buy time, he mused, he had enough money to buy many years of it.

FIFTY SIX

Emmanuel knew he was being tailed by a policeman in plain clothes. It was a condition of being released from police custody to go hunting down the money.

His first port of call was Claude's pitch by Parc Montsouris. Of course, Claude would not know where the suitcase of euros was but he would certainly have witnessed the feverish activity in the park when the banknotes were borne away by the wind.

"*Bon matin, Claude.*"

"*Bon matin, mon ami.*" He recognised the man who regularly dropped coins into his hat when passing.

"Tell me, if you will. Has some generous soul offered you a banknote in the last day or two?"

Claude laughed.

"A banknote? Mon dieu! It would be a fine thing to be offered just a few euros."

Emmanuel smiled and pulled some small change from his pocket. "Here, get yourself a haircut. If anyone should offer you a five-hundred euro banknote inform the police immediately."

Claude laughed again. "I always do, monsieur. I always do!"

It was probably a wise thing he did, after it had grown dark, to return the suitcase to where he had first found it ... behind the recycling bins. He remained curious as to how and why it was there in the first place.

FIFTY SEVEN

Emmanuel had duplicate keys to both the entrance and exit doors of the Paris catacombs. One of its custodians occasionally helped him to identify persons of interest that had sneaked into the vast underground tomb to dodge law enforcement agencies. Fifty euros had paid for a thirty-minute loan of the keys while duplicates were being.

If he could lose the plain-clothes policeman for a few minutes ...

They had reached the catacombs. Now he just needed to cause a distraction.

FIFTY EIGHT

There was once a time when Emmanuel was a talented sprinter. He was a school champion over one hundred metres and in 1997 finished third in the World Schools Athletic Championships in Cherbourg. He had warm memories of crouching nervously on the start line waiting for the official to fire his pistol. In fact, several years later, when he had chosen to set himself up as a private detective, he had purchased a starting pistol and twenty blanks. He still had nineteen remaining, one having been used to frighten a client into paying an overdue bill for services rendered.

He chose a spot close to the locked entrance door to the catacombs, lowered his arm and fired a blank into the ground. Bystanders turned towards him but saw no gun or sign of danger scurried away in terror and sought somewhere that might offer shelter from a terrorist attack.`

There was no terrorist attack, of course. People turned in the direction of the explosive sound but saw no gun, no sign of an imminent attack, nothing they need fear. They might have seen a man lounging against a wall close to the entrance to the catacombs. Emmanuel waited until they had drifted away leaving him with personal space to surreptitiously insert the duplicate key into the lock. A final look to reassure himself that he had lost the police officer that had been tailing him … and then there he was … back among the bones once more.

The police officer had heard the gunshot. People were turning their heads, some appeared frightened but once they realised they were in no danger they had drifted away and gone about their business.

He needed to remove any evidence that could link him to Jeremy's daughter. He took a small brush from a deep pocket inside his black coat and began to retrace the steps he had taken following Annabelle. Fortunately, the group she'd latched on to had shuffled along and kicked up dust that had destroyed most of their footprints. Anything doubtful, he brushed away. It took almost fifty minutes for him to reach the exit door on Avenue René-Coty. Now to make his escape. To change his appearance. To start afresh with a new name. He withdrew the key from his pocket and was about to insert into the lock …

"Stay where you are, monsieur."

Emmanuel hadn't heard the police officer approach from behind.

"Throw your weapon on the ground."

"Weapon? It's a starting pistol. A keepsake. In 1997, I finished third in the World Schools Athletic Championships in Cherbourg."

"And I am the President of France. Turn around, monsieur. Drop the key you must surely have to the ground and then stand with your hands behind your back."

Emmanuel complied. Handcuffs snapped shut on his wrists.

FIFTY NINE

Claude was feeling hungry. He had spent much of the morning at his usual pitch but the people of Paris were not feeling generous that day and there was little loose change in his beret. It must be the new white shirt, he surmised. A beggar in a crisp clean shirt sounded the wrong note … wearing brand new Nike trainers was a mistake, too!

There was a restaurant on Rue d'Alsesia, not that far from his pitch, called 'Zeyer'. He had many times eyed the menu on the board beside the door and envied the diners he saw seated at the tables each covered with white fabric. Forty-seven euros could buy him a three-course meal. Forty-seven euro had seemed a fortune just a week ago but, today, he had a crisp 500 euro note in his pocket ... enough for him to dine as he wished every day that week.

He stooped to pick up his cap. Four euros for five

hours begging! His tummy rumbled. He fingered the bank note. His mind made up, he headed for Zeyer.

As he pushed open the door, several diners glanced his way. A waiter stepped towards him and frowned.

"*Désolée, Monsieur, mais c'est complet.*" I am sorry, sir, but we are full.

Claude put his hand in a trouser pocket and tugged out a 500 euro note.

The waiter stared at it for several long seconds and then looked at Claude.

"We have a late cancellation. There is a table for

you by the window. I hope you will be comfortable and enjoy the view. I will fetch a menu."

The waiter went into the kitchen and said to the chef, "There is a street-beggar seated by the window. He waved a brand new 500 euro note in my face."

The chef peered through a small window in the door kitchen door.

"*C'est Claude!*"

Picking up a menu, the waiter returned to the restaurant and placed it on Claude's table.

"*Je serai de retour dans cinq minutes.*" I will return in five minutes.

Indeed, he did return after about five minutes ... but not with a menu ... with two French police officers,

SIXTY

The police searched Claude's apartment. It didn't take long. They soon found the plastic bags containing banknotes. One of them asked, "How did you come by so many crisp, new 500 euro banknotes?"

"I found them in a suitcase."

"These unused notes bear consecutive serial numbers. They are what people were chasing after across Parc Montsouris. Monsieur Claude, I don't know if you will receive a reward or serve time in prison but I think *we* might be rewarded with a promotion!"

SIXTY ONE

Jeremy's phone rang. He looked at the screen. The call was from his manager at MI6.

"I've received a call from my counterpart in Paris. It seems that most of the money has now been recovered."

"Yes, sir, and once the news gets out it will be difficult for anyone to use the ones that were blown away."

"Indeed. Your daughter is unharmed?"

"Unharmed but still shaken. She has a large

bruise on her head but the hospital says there is no serious damage."

"That, too, is good news. I shall wait until I know just how much money has been returned to the bank before I deduct the balance from your salary."

"Are you telling me ..."

The line had gone dead.

SIXTY TWO

"Do you have the slightest idea where you were taken after Degarmo led you from the café above the Picasso Museum?"

"I'm sorry, dad, but I don't. I think I might

recognise the road and then I'm sure I could identify the house. The journey took around thirty minutes and there were trees shielding it from the road."

Thirty minutes in busy Paris traffic. Two, maybe three miles … in any direction.

"Have you got your phone with you?" Annabelle asked.

"Yes, of course. Why?"

"You should be able to track the location of my phone by using Find my Friends."

"In your rucksack?"

"Yes. It was in the rucksack when I was taken

into the house."

"Good girl! Well done! Let's take a look."

Jeremy took his phone out of his jacket, turned it on, pressed the icon for **Find My**.

"Well, well. Success. It's only about three kilometres from where we are now. I'll flag down a taxi."

"No. I'd rather walk. It won't take that long and I'm not so keen on confined spaces right now."

Jeremy and his daughter had walked for about forty minutes when Annabelle whispered, "this is the street."

SIXTY THREE

"You stand aside. I don't want her to see you when she opens the door."

He pushed a button and heard a 'ding-dong.'

After fifteen or so seconds the door was part-opened and a smartly-dressed woman asked,

"Oui, puis-je vous aider?

"I think my daughter left her phone here. I've come to collect it."

"I think there must be some mistake," the woman said as she began closing the door.

"Really? Well I don't agree. May I come in?"

"*Monsieur ...*"

"It's in the backpack you took from me,"

Annabelle added helpfully as she set a foot in the door.

"*C'est toi!*"

"It certainly is!"

"Emmanuel Degarmo ... is he here?" Jeremy asked.

"*Non, il a été arrêté*".

"He's been arrested? Good. That should speed up our search for him. Now ... my daughter's backpack and phone ... or should I call the police and ask them to search the house?"

"*Reste là une minute,*" the woman said as she

turned and walked towards a cupboard beneath the stairs in the hall.

Jeremy winked at his daughter. She winked back and smiled at her father.

The smile faded after the woman reached into the cupboard and then turned towards them with a pistol in her hand.

SIXTY FOUR

Annabelle leapt to one side, yanking a jacket from off the coat stand in the hallway. She swept it towards the woman. There was a dull explosion as the gun was fired. A bullet lodged itself in the thick padding of the jacket and the woman flayed her arms in an effort to free the gun. She didn't succeed. The last time Jeremy had performed a rugby tackle was on a school playing field almost twenty-five years earlier but urgency saw him hurl himself at the woman's legs. She crashed to the floor … and there was an explosion. She cried out in pain and clutched her arm as she involuntary pulled the gun's trigger. Annabelle bound forward and retrieved the gun.

Jeremy punched **112** into his phone and requested both ambulance and police assistance.

SIXTY FIVE

At least, Annabelle has both her backpack and, more importantly, her phone back. The police and ambulance services had responded swiftly to

Jeremy's phone call.

Emmanuel and the woman were both facing criminal charges but Claude walked away unburdened by any allegations of theft. In fact, the bank hinted at a possible reward coming his way after recovering more than eighty per cent of its money. Businesses were advised to be cautious of anyone offering crisp, new five-hundred-euro notes which, although they continue to be legal tender, were no longer issued after April 2019.

SIXTY SIX

Some customers, but most likely businesses, that held accounts at Banque de France Services faced embarrassment when depositing crisp, new €500 notes and faced questions ... how did you acquire these notes? Do you have you a name? Do you have CCTV of the person making the deposit?

Of concern to both the bank and the police was the whereabouts of both Maurice Garnier, branch manager and Pierre Picard, his deputy.

They were faced with a dilemma. Their self-imposed confinement inside the recycling bins meant that they smelt of rotten food and garden waste ... no way to present themselves to bank customers or their staff. They would be a laughingstock ... and how would they explain away their furtive departure from duties via a side door?

Then there was the question of the suitcase and its contents. What had they intended doing with the money and where was it?

"We need fresh clothes," Garnier said. "And a bath," Picard added. They thought about it for a minute or two, made their decision, and searched on their phones for the nearest swimming pool. They still had their wallets and credit cards so paid for a taxi to take them to a hotel at 55 Rue Boussingault. The hotel had its own swimming pool. The driver sniffed and wrinkled his nose as they climbed in but Garnier pulled a fifty-euro note from his wallet and handed it to him.

"*S'il vous plaît, gardez-le.*" Keep it, please.

The traffic was not heavy and they soon arrived at the hotel on Rue Boussingault.

"If we book ourselves in for the night we can make use of their swimming pool and shower facilities. We might be able to take somebody's clothes from an unlocked locker. We cannot be seen in the dining room stinking of garden rubbish and rotting food."

"If we're caught stealing we could be in trouble," Picard said.

"I think we're already in deep trouble. Once we've settled in, I'll use my phone to check the current whereabouts of the suitcase-full of money. We might still be rich my midnight."

Or facing many years behind bars, Picard silently thought.

"Have you a double room for tonight, Monsieur?"

The receptionist regarded the two smelly, scruffy men with distaste and held out a hand.

"*Avez-vous de l'argent?*"

Garnier pulled a roll of fifty-euro notes from an inside pocket of his smelly jacket.

"*Deux chambres simples, s'il tu plait.*"

"*Certainement messieurs.*" He handed over a pass-key for each room.

They did not go directly to their rooms but headed for the bathing pool.

"We need to find a couple of unlocked lockers containing clean clothes ," Maurice Garnier said.

"But what if we are caught ?"

"I'm sure the police will find us an appropriate change of clothing."

They entered the changing area and split their search between them.

"Maurice ... sir ... there are two open lockers here with clothes and shoes."

Maurice moved across one aisle.

"*C'est bon*. Let's see how they are for size."

They both pulled out clothing and shoes and slipped into separate changing rooms. A few minutes passed.

First to appear was Pierre Picard wearing blue denim jeans, a sporty tee-shirt and trainers. They were all a surprisingly good fit. At least, they were for Pierre although the trousers were ten centimetres short revealing a pair of mismatched socks. The shoes were at least three sizes too large and he kept slipping out of them.

Maurice, however, was not as fortunate.

The clothing found in the second locker comprised a pair of skimpy shorts, a tee-shirt with **'KISS ME- I'M FRENCH'** across the chest and a floppy white sun hat.

"Monsieur Garnier, you must never walk into our

bank dressed like that."

"I think it highly unlikely I'll ever walk into any bank again and certainly not with 500 euro notes stuffed into the pockets," Maurice grunted. "Anyway, as soon as we get settled into our rooms we must take one of the notes to buy some more appropriate clothing."

They exited the changing rooms and tried slipping surreptitiously into the corridor.

They were halfway between their rooms and the stairwell leading down to the dining room when a voice piped up from beneath them.

"Monsieur Garnier and Pierre Picard! Well, this must be my lucky day. I hadn't expected to see find you here. I called at your bank this morning in search of a loan. They told me you were both busy. Well, I can see that you have, indeed, been busy … out buying new outfits by the look of you both."

"Non, non!" Pierre stammered. "These are not our clothes. They belong to someone else."

"Really? Well, I'll keep an eye out for them. They shouldn't be too difficult to spot. Just as well for them it's a warm afternoon, eh, monsieurs ?"

The man continued along the corridor chuckling to himself.

"I think we should put off eating until we've been out and purchased clothes more becoming of senior bank executives."

"And shoes that fit properly!" Pierre added.

SIXTY SEVEN

"They are one hundred and eighty euros, *messieurs, s'il vous plait*."

Pierre took a crisp 500 euro note from a pocket of his ill-fitting trousers.

The shop assistant regarded the note for several seconds.

"This has come straight from the bank, oui? It is beautiful."

Pierre nodded.

"I will wrap your clothes and find suitable bags for them," the assistant said. "I'll only be a couple of minutes," he said as he set off towards the back of the store.

He walked back and through an arch that led to a packing area at the back of the shop and was lost to view … which was as well because the two senior bank officials would have taken to their heels … and mismatched socks.

Pierre Picard pricked up his ears when he caught the end of a conversation … " it looks as though it's come straight off the press," he heard.

" Yes, it has watermarks and a regular serial number … yes, I will try to keep them here."

"*Monsieurs*," he said as he re-entered the shop with their package. "May I show you some of our latest fashions?" His voice faded along with his fake smile when he discovered that he had returned to an empty shop.

Once outside on the boulevard, Maurice Garnier shoved his hand into the small of his deputy's back.

"Police will put shops and restaurants on alert. Our pictures will make newspaper headlines. We must alter our appearance and change the 500-euro notes for smaller denominations."

"How will we do that, sir?"

"We will start by opening new bank accounts for

ourselves ... but not with BNP Paribas, of course."

SIXTY EIGHT

Le Préfet de police addressed Degarmo. "Emmanuel Degarmo, I am offering you an opportunity to ingratiate yourself with the authorities in exchange for your experience and assistance in tracking down Maurice Garnier, the former manager and Pierre Picard, the former deputy manager of Banque de France, 9 Rue Croix des Petits Champs."

"But we robbed the bank of two million euros. There was a suitcase stuffed full of notes. We left it behind the recycling bins by Parc Montsouris for Monsieur Roberts to collect. We cannot know for certain who took it before we had climbed into the bins to hide.

"Claude took the case to his apartment," le Préfet de police stated. "You know of Claude? He begs from a pitch close to the park. We recovered it. A few notes were missing ... swept away by the wind ... but, no doubt, some shopkeeper or other will report having been handed one. "

"You could receive a reduced sentence when you eventually appear before a judge."

"Could?"

"I cannot promise anything."

"I need photographs of the two men."

Le Préfet shrugged his shoulders.

"I do have their passports but ... hey! ... the bank most likely have them on its security system. That would be a good place to start. I'll even lend you one of my cars and an officer to make your journey quicker but I can't promise you a return ride."

"I know my way around Paris, monsieur."

"Be sure not to leave Paris. I want to know where you are at all times."

"You're attaching me to a dog lead, perhaps?"

"A tracking device attached to your ankle. Please do not misuse it. If I discover it's taken a trip into the Seine, I might lose any inclination I might have to assist you at a later date."

"I will need some money," Degarmo said. "Taxis. Food. Maybe a little bribery among my associates."

"I will ensure you are well-prepared. You have a reputation for out-beating my gendarmes when it comes to finding someone we have an interest in. On this occasion, I hope you live up to it."

Degarmo waved to the driver as he left him by the entrance to the bank and sped back to the police station.

SIXTY NINE

"I am Emmanuel Degarmo"

"*Monsieur* ... we are expecting you. Please follow me."

He was led to the far side of the bank to an office door marked *directeur*.

"Emmanuel! I have photos of the two men you are seeking. Perhaps I should ask to be released from my duties to assist you in your search."

"Ha! An excellent idea but I daresay you're of my use here keeping an eye out for 500€ notes although I rather doubt Garnier or Picard will drop in to say *bonjour*."

"I rather much doubt it, too. Here, take these. We have a policy here of taking staff photos each year. Hairstyles change. Beards grow. We all become older. Impersonations to gain access to our vaults are impossible. Two other members of staff have to confirm the verity of anyone entering them.

Garnier picked up the photos, examined them closely and then tucked them into the inside pocket of his jacket.

"I will return the photos to you once I have delivered the two men to *Le Préfet de police*."

"Tell me, Emmanuel ... what do you receive in exchange for locating Maurice and Pierre?"

"A lighter sentence, I hope!"

SEVENTY

Garnier stood outside a small lettings agency on Avenue Phillipe Auguste in the Bastille area of

Paris.

This was as good a place to start as any.

"*Bon matin. Je suis Emmanuel Degarmo.* I am a private detective and *Le Préfet de police* has tasked me with finding two employees of the BNP Paribas."

The young lady sitting behind a desk stood up.

"Please ... one moment. I will fetch my manager."

A minute or so later she returned with a dapper young man.

Emmanuel took the two photos from his pocket.

"I am a private investigator and *Le Préfet de police* has asked me to help find the whereabouts of these two gentlemen. They must be *somewhere* and are higher unlikely to be sleeping on the streets. They have money and will need a place to stay. I am asking letting agencies if they have rented a property to them."

The manager studied the photos.

"I recognise them!" he exclaimed.

Garnier could hardly believe his luck.

"That's wonderful! Where can I find them?"

"I've no idea," the manager confessed. "I saw their pictures in *Le Monde* yesterday. They have not been here."

Garnier sighed.

"*Merci*. If they should visit here please let me know." Garnier took a calling card from his jacket.

"Certainly. I am sorry I cannot help you further."

Garnier left the agency and began walking back towards the nearest metro station. At the same time that he boarded a train, a bearded man in an old, peaked cap entered the letting agency.

"Do you have a two-bedroom apartment available to rent away from busy streets and the Paris crowds?" he asked.

The female assistant told him such properties were in short supply at the present time and asked him what he was willing to pay.

"It doesn't matter," the bearded man replied.

The assistant scrolled through properties on her lap and after a minute or so looked up.

"We have an apartment new in this morning on Avenue Phillipe Auguste in the Bastille district of Paris. It is a two-bedroomed apartment on the third floor. The rent is 2495 euros payable one month in advance."

"I'll take it!"

He hated using his own money. He and Pierre should have had a suitcase stuffed full of 500€ notes to pay the trifling sum of the deposit. Five notes would have covered it with 5€ change.

The assistant accepted his cheque, unlocked a

metal wall cupboard and withdrew two keys. She handed them to the bearded man who then left the agency and walked away briskly.

"What a scruffy beard!" she thought to herself.

SEVENTY ONE

The woman was still wearing dark glasses although the sun had hidden itself behind dark, gathering clouds. She had read in a newspaper that a reward was being offered for information leading to the whereabouts of the two bank employees. She regretted rendering Annabelle unconscious but it was what Emmanuel had instructed her to do.

Annabelle had been dragged to his waiting car and bundled on to the back seat but where had he taken her? She had no idea. What she *did* know, however was the address of Emmanuel's home in Paris.

SEVENTY TWO

Maurice Garnier removed his mobile phone from a jacket pocket and opened the *Find me* app to locate the present position of the suitcase. He was aware of the fact the street beggar, Claude, had emptied most of its contents into plastic bags that he had taken from a supermarket but he had another use in mind for the abandoned suitcase.

The tracking device was still in place! His

phone's screen zoomed in to display its location.

Garnier began walking towards the Paris catacombs and the recycling bins. Surely, the suitcase hadn't gone undiscovered. Of course not! Claud had found it, managed to break it open and then stuff banknotes into the plastic bags before returning to his apartment. That is what must have happened ... in which case, there was still money to be found.

SEVENTY THREE

The same thoughts were running through the mind of Maurice Garnier.

"Pierre ... I think we should check whether the suitcase has been moved."

"That would be an unnecessary risk, Maurice ... er... sir."

"We're already in a high-risk predicament so I don't think adding to it slightly will compromise our futures to any greater extent."

"The bank will be keen to bring us to justice," Pierre said.

"And no doubt their wish will be granted ... eventually. Meanwhile, I've already spent 2,495 euros of my own money and I would much prefer to be spending someone else's."

"Of course, sir. You're quite right ... just as you always are."

SEVENTY FOUR

As the two bank employees drew near to the recycling bins, Pierre Picard blurted out, "I am *not* climbing into the bins again whatever the circumstances!"

"But you had acquired such a fragrant scent when you climbed back out!"

Pierre kept his lips sealed but eventually felt persuaded to remark, "I cannot imagine what you hope to find."

"I am hoping that not far from the recycling bins we will find Claude."

"Claude?" asked Pierre.

"The beggar who has a pitch close to *Parc Montsouris*. Not far, in fact, from the Paris catacombs."

SEVENTY FIVE

The woman in dark glasses rang the front doorbell of Emmanuel's apartment. She did not expect him to appear. He was always out and about on business and when at home was wary of callers at his door. She smiled into the security camera that connected to the doorbell, waved a hand and walked away.

Phone calls to his office on Avenue Marceau went unanswered and were met with a rapid, repetitive beeping sound signifying that the number was either temporarily unavailable or permanently disconnected. He was not answering his mobile either. Calls went to voicemail.

Emmanuel Degarmo was not an easy person to contact when he chose not to be.

SEVENTY SIX

As it happened, Emmanuel wanted to speak to the woman in dark glasses. He needed a place to stay for a day or two away from his own apartment which he imagined was under close scrutiny. If he was lucky, the beggar Claude might still have a plastic bag or two of bank notes that the police had not discovered when they raided his house ... if he could get his hands on them he might flee

Paris with sufficient money to start anew elsewhere.

He took out his phone and tapped in the number of his accomplice ... a woman who liked to wear dark glasses.

SEVENTY SEVEN

"Emmanuel! I've been trying to contact you," she said. "I would like more of the money I helped you steal. Bear in mind that I was your accomplice in the kidnapping and entombment of the English girl. The police will eventually discover my involvement. I need to move well away from Paris."

Emmanuel smiled to himself. How convenient

that she wished to meet up with him. That could easily be arranged.

"I hid some of the money in the Paris catacombs," he lied. "That is where we took Jeremy's daughter. That is where we dumped her body." At least, *that* much was true.

"Are you in that area at the moment?" the woman asked.

"I can easily reach the catacombs within fifteen minutes," Emmanuel assured her.

"Then I will meet you there. Please wait for me. We can enter through the main door to the catacombs and sneak out unnoticed by the rear exit onto Avenue du Colonel Henri Rol-Tanguy."

"That is a good plan. I will be waiting for you."

SEVENTY EIGHT

Maurice Garnier, former manager of BNP Paribas, and his former deputy, Pierre Picard, took a right turn onto Avenue Phillipe Auguste.

Taking a key from his jacket pocket he turned to Pierre and smiled.

"Another minute or two and we can relax inside our new temporary home."

Pierre turned to look over his shoulder.

"It looks as though we were not followed so we're off to a good start."

"A good *start* but not the best. We must stay out

of sight as much as possible."

Pierre brushed his chin.

"When my new beard is as bushy as yours nobody will recognise us."

Maurice stopped suddenly and pointed. There was a gendarme standing by the entrance to the apartment block.

"Keep walking. I doubt he knows who we are but it might make him curious if we suddenly turn around."

"Good morning, officer." Maurice smiled politely and held out the key to the apartment. "Time to rest our weary legs."

"I wish I could do the same," the gendarme replied ruefully. "Been on my feet all morning. Somebody has reported their dog missing on the Avenue and I've been ordered to find it."

"Is that what is now expected of our police force?"

"The dog in question belongs to a friend of my *Lieutenant de police*. Finding lost dogs has priority over catching criminals, it seems."

Maurice nodded sympathetically. "And there are plenty of *them* to be caught!"

"*Oui, monsieur.*"

*

SEVENTY NINE

"How is business today?" the manager of the letting agency asked.

"Just one new rental," his female assistant replied. "He took the apartment on Avenue Phillipe Auguste."

"The two-bedroomed apartment? Is he sharing?"

"I don't know. He didn't say."

"It's not important. What matters is that his cheque doesn't bounce. Did he mention what he did for a living?"

"No ... but I think he must be doing well for himself. He paid with 500€ notes."

The manager looked surprise.

"*Mon dieu!*" he exclaimed. "Did they look new?"

"Well, yes. They were not wrinkled or worn in any obvious way."

"Stay there one moment while I fetch the newspaper from my office."

He returned within twenty seconds and spread it over the counter.

"I want to show you a picture." He flicked over several pages and then pointed at an item at the top of page three. "Could he have been this man?"

"Definitely not. The man had a beard ... a scruffy

beard ... but perhaps he was still growing it."

"Imagine him without the beard ... do you think he might look like *this*?"

She studied the picture in the newspaper for a while.

"The nose, the mouth and the high cheekbones look very similar," she finally said. "Who am I looking at?"

"If I told you, you'd laugh in my face."

"Try me."

"Maurice Garnier. The manager of BNP Paribas on L'Avenue des Champs-Élysées."

EIGHTY

Emmanuel tapped his foot impatiently as he stood at the entrance to the Paris catacombs. He felt certain that the woman in dark glasses was expecting a share of whatever money she imagined he had secured for himself. Well, he thought wryly, she could expect a share of precisely nothing!

"Emmanuel!"

He turned swiftly as she tapped his shoulder from behind.

"Can you guess why I'm here?" she asked.

"You think I should be dispensing some money

for your assistance in abducting the English girl, no doubt."

"Correct ... and for my being an accessory to your murder of her in the catacombs."

"But how can you be certain I carried out such a dastardly crime?"

"Because, Emmanuel, you are professional in all you undertake. It is why you have such a distinguished reputation in your field of work."

Emmanuel smiled. "And you believe flattery will earn you a share of any money you think I might have misappropriated?"

"Better that flattery is successful rather than a bullet to your brain," the woman said as she revealed the small gun resting in the grip of her hand.

"The money is hidden in the catacombs," he lied.

"That is why I suggested we meet here."

"So ... you still have a key to unlock the entrance door?"

"I have ... an arrangement with one of the custodians."

"Just how much money have you hidden in the catacomb?"

"Sufficient for you to travel abroad if the fancy should take you."

"What is it like in there ... in the catacombs ...

I've never felt brave enough to enter."

"There are bones. Lots of bones. More than you can ever imagine. Piles of them ... and skulls ... but their eye sockets are empty so nobody will notice us."

The woman shuddered. "I have brought a torch."

"You will need it. I have one, too. Quite powerful. There are lights but they are usually switched on only when tours take place."

"Okay ... well, let's get this over with. You *will* leave the door unlocked?"

"That would not be wise now, would it?" Emmanuel said. "You never know who might chance their luck on a free tour of the passages."

Emmanuel unlocked the entrance door.

"Take care when you enter. There are one hundred and thirty one steps to descend and they can be slippery."

"*Now* you tell me!" she hissed. "I am not wearing trainers. These shoes have no grip."

"Use your torch to guide you. Come now ... we're wasting time."

Emmanuel was agile and knew what to expect. In his haste, he had forgotten to lock the door behind him and after descending twenty or so steps he turned to look back. The woman was still huddled against the rail beside the first step, clutching it with one hand while holding her handbag in the other.

"Hurry up!" he called out.

"I can't! I'm afraid!"

He climbed back up the steps and took her arm.

"Slowly now. You want some money from me? Then show me some courage in return. And take off your sunglasses! You won't need them down here."

She took another tentative step.

"Here - take my arm," Emmanuel said.

She reached out a hand. Emmanuel took hold of it and *tugged hard.* She stumbled, slipped, cried out and tumbled down the steps.

Emmanuel smiled to himself as he covered the remaining distance to where she lay motionless.

He walked past her. One pace ... two ... three ...and then stood frozen as he heard her cry out ...

"You swine ..." The woman moaned.

He frowned and began turning towards her. As he did so, she reached a blooded hand into her handbag and withdrew the pistol she had used to strike Annabelle.

The first shot struck his knee and he collapsed to the ground. The second shot was fired from ground level and grazed his ear narrowly missing his head.

He edged towards her on all fours. She tried to

raise the pistol but this time her strength failed her. Emmanuel gathered his remaining resources and lunged forward with arms outspread. He snatched the pistol from her hand, held it to her head and fired. One more skull for the Paris Catacombs. Now he just needed to drag himself up the one hundred and thirty one steps to the entry door that he had forgotten to lock.

EIGHTY ONE

The police car drove into the Bastille area of Paris and came to a halt as it drew level with the lettings agency on Avenue Phillipe Auguste.

Both front doors opened and two officers with guns protruding from holsters attached to their belts entered the agency.

Once inside, one of the officers took two photos from his jacket pocket and placed them on the counter.

"These are two men we are searching for ... taken before either of them had added any facial hair to their features."

The manager of the agency stared at the photos and tried to visualise them with beards or moustaches.

He shook his head but called out to his female assistant. She stepped from an office at the rear of the building.

"Did you call me?"

"These two officers are looking for *these* two men."

"Those are the men whose pictures appeared in the paper."

"Indeed. Yesterday, one of our officers, who was searching for ... a missing dog ... encountered two men entering an apartment here on Avenue Phillipe Auguste. Upon reflection, he felt there was something vaguely familiar about their features although he thinks they might have disguised their appearance by adding facial hair and swapping smart suits for grubby clothing. Perhaps it is a coincidence that the apartment block they entered is on the very same street as your agency ..."

"A man in dirty clothing and a scruffy beard paid for a month's rent in advance on an apartment a couple of days ago," the assistant offered. "I was most surprised when he paid in cash."

"With bank notes?" the second officer asked.

"Indeed. Lots of them. Two and a half thousand euros and all in crisp new fifty-euro notes."

EIGHTY TWO

Maurice Garnier, manager ... *former* manager ... of BNP Paribas, was growing increasingly concerned about his former and equally disgraced deputy, Pierre Picard. Pierre was increasingly showing signs of panic and had even hinted at surrendering himself to *le Préfet de police de*

Paris. Garnier could not allow that to happen. Garnier *would* not allow that to happen. He preferred the fresh air and open countryside to a gloomy cell whose only view would be of *other* cells and other inmates.

He pushed aside the duvet, climbed out of bed and hurriedly got dressed. He put an ear to the door of the adjoining bedroom and heard the rhythmic snoring of Pierre. Almost perfect. There were locks to each bedroom operated by identical keys. Maurice inserted one of the keys into the door of Pierre's room and turned it clockwise.

He tucked a bundle of newspapers under his arm and walked across the room to the area set aside for a kitchenette, hesitated by the electric hob to view the controls and then pressed and turned the burner knob counterclockwise and waited for it to glow red. Within moments of laying a newspaper across the red-hot hob, it began to smoulder. Seconds later, it burst into flames. Maurice piled more paper on top of the flames. The burning newspapers fell to the floor and the carpeted area soon began to burn. Flames edged towards the curtains. They caught fire. It was time to leave.

EIGHTY THREE

Emmanuel Degarmo clawed his way up the steps. He tried to keep count, each step more challenging than its predecessor. Each step draining his remaining energy. Each step stained with blood from his head wound. For once, he was grateful for his memory lapse. If could only claw his way back up the steps, he would find the door unlocked with its key still in his pocket. Crawl out. Lock the door. Call for help. Claim he had been attacked from behind as he was passing the nearby recycling bins.

The custodian of the Paris Catacombs had arrived fifteen minutes early for his end-of-day inspection of the catacombs and was delighted to find that the local key-smith had already carried out the work and was packing away his tools.

"I hope you are pleased," he said. "The new lock you asked me to fit is stronger and more secure than the old one."

"I certainly hope so. It had served me well over the years but was showing its age. There were signs of rust and it was often a pain to unlock," the custodian acknowledged.

"You'll find the new mechanism is as smooth as the hair on your head."

"But I'm bald!"

"So you are! I'll hand you these three keys and be on my way. Any problems, don't hesitate to give me a call."

"Oh, I'll certainly do that!"

The man walked towards his van, turned, raised his hand, started the engine and drove away.

The custodian checked the door was locked and put the keys into his pocket. For once, he would assume all was as it should be in the catacombs. He was feeling tired. Kept awake half the night by loud music from nearby neighbours. This was a day when the catacombs were not open to the public so he felt he could slip away home and nobody would be any the wiser.

EIGHTY FOUR

Emmanuel Degarmo clutched his damaged ear, winced and dragged his crippled leg another couple of steps towards the door. He had lost count of the number of steps he had hauled his body but, raising his chin, estimated no more than five remained. He tried doing the sum in his head ... one hundred and thirty one less five ... his head throbbed and another drop of blood dropped from his damaged ear and soaked his sodden shirt. His carefully manicured fingernails were cracked ... maybe four more steps.

The high-low wail of fire engines penetrated the dark, damp catacombs but Degarmo was too occupied with his own exertions and pain to feel concern for some cat stuck up a tree.

Maybe three more steps. The damp air of the catacombs was drawn into his nose and his throat stung as the fustiness was sucked into his lungs.

EIGHTY FIVE

A small crowd had begun to gather at a safe distance from the apartment block on Avenue Phillipe Auguste. The street had been closed on either side of the block and neighbouring tenants had been evacuated from their buildings.

Maurice Garnier stood within that small crowd and could feel himself tremble. In due course, the lettings agency would no doubt confirm that the rooms in which the fire originated had been rented to two gentlemen ... gentlemen whose pictures had recently appeared in newspapers ... gentlemen being hunted by law enforcement agencies. In due course when one, but not two, bodies were removed from the burning building, the hunt for a man with a shabby beard would be intensified.

The police had cordoned off the avenue from both directions while the firemen dealt with the remaining flickers of flames and were ushering those within the cordon to the side of the road.

Maurice was being shepherded towards the far pavement when one of the officers placed a hand on his shoulder and cried out, *"Stay where you are!"*

Maurice turned and instantly recognised the officer. It was the one that had been standing outside the apartment block searching for the dog that belonged to a friend of the *Lieutenant*.

He made to run but other bystanders were in his way.

"*Stay where you are!*" A second officer joined his colleague and grabbed Maurice's arms as the first officer clamped cuffs over his wrists.

EIGHTY SIX

Emmanuel Degarmo breathed a sigh of relief. He had little enough breath left after climbing the final few steps so he treasured it. He twisted a shoulder and reached into his pocket for the key to the catacombs door. It door should still be as he had left it. Unlocked. Should the custodian have passed by to check the door, and found it unlocked, he would put it down to the carelessness or forgetfulness of the man who paid him for the duplicate key that gained him unauthorised entry for ... goodness knows what? Maybe he thought the private detective was storing something in a place he assumed nobody would ever look. Whatever the reason, what trouble could he possibly cause?

Emmanuel raised himself up on to one leg and grabbed hold of the door handle. He held it tightly and, balancing on his single good leg, fumbled in his pocket and extracted the duplicate key. He inserted it into the lock ... and frowned. He wriggled it. Removed and reinserted it again but the internal mechanism rendered the key ineffective. *This could not be!* He tried again ...

and again. The result was the same.

He was trapped amongst the bones of the Paris catacombs with a damaged knee and the body of a woman he had murdered.

EIGHTY SEVEN

Pierre Picard survived the fire. He had been awoken by the smell of burning and immediately found himself choking on the smoke that filled his nose and throat and lungs. His eyes watered and stung. He scrambled out of bed and staggered across the floor towards the bedroom door. He reached out and grasped the handle *but the door didn't open!* He shook the door and tugged on the handle but, of course, it didn't magically open.

His mobile phone was on a bedside table and he tapped out **1 8** to connect with the fire brigade. He opened the bedroom window and took gulps of fresh air.

Smoke began creeping beneath the door. He could hear items falling and smashing to the floor in the adjoining lounge. He stood beside the window and peered down at the small crowd of pedestrians that had gathered on the pavement below.

He heard the sirens of police cars growing louder and then the more distant wailings of fire trucks.

Six police officers leapt from their cars and began forming a cordon around the growing crowd as it was pushed back on to the sidewalk.

Pierre stared at the spectators and his eyes homed in on an arrest that was being made. A man was being handcuffed ... *and yes ... he was certain that man was Maurice Garnier!*

EIGHTY EIGHT

Emmanuel Degarmo sat exhausted on the one hundred and thirty first step leading to the exit door. He was trapped. He had three options.

He could use his phone to summon help or he could limp back down and crawl one and a half kilometres to the exit door on Avenue René-Coty ... which was probably locked, too. He winced, clutched his knee and ruled that out. The third option was to remain where he was and wait until a guide opened up to take a tourist group into the catacomb's vast network of tunnels and countless millions of bones.

He shifted his position slightly to remove his phone. He stared at it thoughtfully. Call for help? Wait for a tourist group? The decision was made for him when he opened his phone to a blank screen. The battery had run down.

EIGHTY NINE

The firemen set up an aerial ladder platform lift that enabled them to rapidly gain access to the third floor apartment from which Pierre Picard was half-leaning out of its wide window. He had a fear of heights, still more so of falling from the third-floor apartment. All thoughts of Maurice Garnier and the police faded as he was assisted from the window and lifted on to the platform. He closed his eyes an gripped the rail hard as the platform was slowly lowered.

The journey was quickly over and Pierre was helped back on to the pavement. Unfortunately, his relief ended right there. Two police officers were waiting for him. As one fastened handcuffs to his wrists the other commented,

"Your journey is not quite over, monsieur, but do not worry. We have a car laid on especially for you."

Pierre didn't need telling but the second officer made it plain.

"Save your excuses and explanations until we reach *le commissariat de police.*"

NINETY

Emmanuel Degamo had a phone with an exhausted battery but he still had a watch with a little battery life remaining.

The information on the watch's screen told him that it was eleven-thirty in the evening and that the date was Thursday November the second, 2025. Just how long had he been trapped in the catacombs? The dim, damp surrounding made him shiver ... not from the conditions but from the knowledge that he was presently a prisoner of the catacombs and that he was surrounded by the bones of at least six million former mortals. Had any of them ever been trapped as he now was, waiting impatiently and anxiously for a custodian to unlock a door?

He had been here on many occasions for various reasons, some good, some more sinister, and had even put names to some of the grinning skulls as though he was greeting old friends.

What time did the catacombs open in the morning? He ought to know. The catacombs were open to the public on six days, from Tuesday to Sunday, and entry was between 9.45 am to 8.30 pm. with the last entry at 7:30 PM. He would have to remain captive in the catacombs for another eleven hours, without food, water or the comforting warmth of his luxurious bed.

NINETY ONE

Jeremy Roberts opened his phone and tapped out an encrypted message to his manager at Vauxhall Cross, the London, headquarters of MI6's Secret Intelligence Service.

'Returning to England with my daughter on a flight from Charles de Gaulle Airport tomorrow morning. Will contact you once we have landed to arrange a meeting. Search under way for Emmanuel Degamo. Most of the money has been recovered.'

NINETY TWO

The seconds and minutes passed ... and then the hours crept by and Emmanuel Degamo was shivering. His shirt and jacket did little to create warmth in his dank surroundings. He had no way of summoning help as his phone battery had died hours ago ... and then his ears pricked up. There was light hammering on the entrance door. He tried standing but his knee gave way and he cried out in pain. Help was at hand on the far side of the door ... just a step or two away.

The hammering ceased. Degamo held his breath ... and waited.

A passer-by was attracted to the sound of light

hammering and was curious to know what was being pinned to the entrance door to the catacombs. As the custodian moved away, the passer-by moved closer.

Ah, yes! He had seen that poster before. It was probably fixed to the door every year to provide information to would-be visitors.

'The catacombs will reopen next year in April 2026 after undergoing major renovation and modernisation.'

NINETY THREE

'Delighted to hear about you daughter. I trust she was worth two million euros. How long will it take you to repay the money? Do not ask me to

raise your salary!' Please drop by Vauxhall Cross HQ as soon as convenient for debriefing.'

NINETY FOUR

Five months later ...

The Paris catacombs reopened to the public. There had been a sensational story in newspapers and on television channels.

The bodies of two Parisians had been discovered in a gruesome state. The emaciated remains of Maurice Garnier, a prominent private investigator, lay on the steps leading down into the catacombs.

Not far from where he lay, a second body, that of a young woman, was spreadeagled across the path with a bullet hole in her head. Beside her was a pair of dark sunglasses.

NINETY FIVE

Claude stood at his usual spot close to Parc Montsouris. The morning had been kind to him and his cap was filled with loose euros and a note or two. He had no need of the money but he liked to acknowledge his regular patrons as they passed by. He had no friends to speak of other than fellow beggars but they occupied their own pitches and avoided infringing the pitches of others.

The police and the banks had no way of knowing just how many five-hundred euro notes had blown away in the wind. Claude had filled plastic bags with the bulk of the money and taken them back to his apartment. The police had searched his premises and taken away two bags stuffed with notes that had been stored in a wardrobe. Claude had neglected to mention a *third* plastic bag of money that he had tucked behind one of the recycling bins close to the entrance to the Paris catacombs.

NINETY SIX

Charlotte and Louise were both six-year old girls who liked to play in *Le Parc Montsouris*. One of their favourite games was hide-and-seek.

"You must turn around and count to twenty and

no peeking," Charlotte insisted. She looked around for a place to hide and when she was satisfied that Louise wasn't cheating she dashed towards the recycling bins, squeezed in behind the one closest to her and sat down on a soft plastic bag.

"Coming!" Louise called out. "Ready or not!"

Several minutes passed and Louise hadn't discovered Charlotte's hiding place. Charlotte began to grow impatient and stood up. Overcome by curiosity she prodded the bag with a twig. It was soft and didn't smell of anything horrible. The bag split slightly and a piece of crisp, colourful paper poked out of the hole she had made. She tugged it free and read the large number printed at the top. '**500**'. There was a circle of stars and funny drawings, too. Then she heard Louise's voice again.

"I know you're behind the bins because I can see your foot sticking out but mummy says I'm not to go too close to them because they have germs."

Charlotte stepped to one side and waved the piece of paper.

"Look what I found!" she exclaimed excitedly and held up a 500 euro banknote,

"There's a whole bag full of these. We could use them to play '*shop*'."

NINETY SEVEN

Claude left his apartment and walked towards *Le Parc Montsouris*, entered, and made his way to the recycling bins. What should he have for dinner? Which swish restaurant should he choose?

As he approached the bins, he spotted two young girls with skipping ropes and waved at them as he passed. Claude was a familiar figure to them and they waved back in return. He failed to see the plastic bag obscured by the trunk of a large oak tree.

When he felt certain that nobody was paying him any attention, he ambled towards the bins. One more look over his shoulder. When he turned back, his eyes opened wide and his smile wilted. *The bag of money was not there!*

NINETY EIGHT

Young Charlotte's mother stared at the bag of money.

"Where did you find this?" she asked.

"Behind a bin in the park!"

"I hope you're telling me the truth. I'd be horrified to think you robbed a bank!"

Charlotte giggled.

"I *am* telling you the truth," she said.

"Well, let's see if we can find a nice policeman to

talk to."

NINETY NINE

Claude went without a fancy meal that day and also the days that followed. He shuffled to his old begging spot by *Parc Montsouris* and lay his worn cap on the pavement. Next, he took the piece of worn cardboard from his knapsack and lay it on the pavement beside him.

'*Pour mangers s'il vous plait.* For food, please.'

ONE HUNDRED

When the Paris catacombs reopened the following April, long queues quickly formed. The catacombs attracted the curious and the ghoulish eager to see the place where the murders had taken place. It added meat to the bones of its sinister reputation in a manner of speaking. The guides had been told not to refer to the grisly events that had taken place the previous November so visitors had to be content with a detailed explanation of the history of the catacombs and its bones.

It usually took about an hour, perhaps a little longer, to complete the tour, eventually reaching the exit at 21 bis, Avenue René-Coty.

ONE HUNDRED and ONE

Jeremy entered Thames House and knocked on

the door of his manager's office.

"Come!"

He opened the door opened and was warmly greeted by his manager who beckoned him to a seat.

"Well, well! Did you enjoy your French holiday?"

"It was hardly that, sir."

"The French authorities tell me that they eventually expect to recover about two thirds of the money and there is a possibility that, in due course, the balance could be retrieved from DeGarmo's estate."

There was a pause that lasted almost twenty

seconds.

"Anyway ... well done. You've handled matters well. You couldn't have done any better ... in the circumstances."

"Thank you, sir."

"I think that's all I have to say for the time being ... except ... I may have an opening for you in a more senior role before long."

"Thank you, sir."

"No promises."

"No, sir."

Jeremy made to leave and had reached the door. "And tell your daughter to take more care in future. There are some wicked people on the streets."

"One thing, sir … Degarmo's son."

"Don't worry about him, Jeremy. I believe he's already being escorted back to France … after a brief visit to A & E. It appears he had a fall and broke his nose."

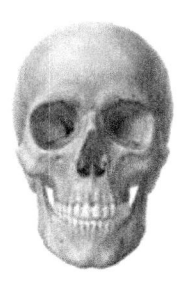

BOOKS FOR YOUNG READERS

Whiskers, Wings and Bushy Tails

(Tales from The Undermead Woods)

An Original series of storybooks for children

Larger print and double-line spacing .

Stories include:

The Inner Mystic Circle

The Race

Curly Cat

Dotty Dormouse

Blackberry Pie George and the Magic

Jigsaw Rain! Rain! Rain!

Where is Dotty Dormouse?

Tap! Tap! Tap!

SwaggerWagger

Three Wheels and a Bell

The Chase

Blackberry Bluff

Rebellion

Autumn

Quiz Night

Black as Night

Sheepish Singing Sisters Links of Gold

Ollie Owl's Experiment (Part Two)

Good Deeds and Evil Intentions

The New Age of Barter

The Mouse That Scored

Buttercups and Daisies

The Tick-Tock 'Tective Agency and the Case of The Missing Tiddles

The Mysterious Case of the Missing Scarecrow

Carrots

Woof! Woof!   (Percy Pigeon is behaving strangely ... once again... and Ollie Owl is determined to use his wisdom and the academic books on the shelves of his library, to correct matters for the citizens (the whiskered, winged, and bushytailed of Undermead.)

Bollington – The Cheshire Cat that Lost Its Grin

Millie Manx (The Tale of a Tail)

Granddad Remembers (but is he telling the truth?)

Ninky and Nurdle (Stories from Noodle-Land)

The Playground of Dreams

What Can I Do When It's Raining Outside?

Buggy Babes

INHABITANTS OF UNDERMEAD include:

Bad Boy Badger and The Snooty Ooty Gang, Dotty Dormouse, Ollie Owl, Percy Pigeon, Doctor Deer O'Dear, Tommy Tortoise, Sammy Snail. SwaggerWagger (a Japanese Chin dog), Richard Robin, Harold Hare, Ferdinand Fox, Wriggly Worm, The Home for Retired Rats and Other Rodents, The Undermead Nuts and Fruit Shop mother and son, Spindly Spider, Ebenezer Eagle, Lord Hawley, Richard Robin,

Farmer Giles, The Big House children, The Scarecrow, The Sheepish Singing Sisters, Henrietta Hedgehog, Happy Hedgehog, Roland Rabbit, Curly Cat.

CRIME

Time to Kill

Stage Fright

The Potato Eaters / Revolving Doors (Fiction based on fact)

Donald Dangle is on The Point of Murder

Black Pad - The Sad Story of Nicola Payne

Friday the Thirteenth

The Woman Across the Road

A TWIST IN THE TALE

Open Pandora's Box and what will you find?

A Night at the Castle   (15 stories with 'a twist in the tale')

Baby Jane

The Little Bedroom

Bulls Eye

A Problem at School

A Running Joke

The Cure

Old Rocker

The New Appointment

The Sunflower

The Christmas Fairy

Pressure

Promotion

Knock, Knock, Knock

The Letter

ROMANCE

The Man from Blue Anchor

www.noteablemusic.co.uk (songs and stories)

Amazon/books/terence braverman

Amazon/kindle/terence braverman

Google/books/terence braverman

terry@terrybraverman.co.uk

Printed in Dunstable, United Kingdom